DELPHY ROSE

DELPHY ROSE

THE GIRL WHO WROTE SONGS

Tina Cathleen MacNaughton

Matador
Unit E2 Airfield Business Park,
Harrison Road, Market Harborough,
Leicestershire. LE16 7UL
Tel: 0116 2792299
Email: books@troubador.co.uk
Web: www.troubador.co.uk/matador
Twitter: @matadorbooks

ISBN 978 1803136 561

British Library Cataloguing in Publication Data.
A catalogue record for this book is available from the British Library.

Printed and bound in the UK by TJ Books Limited, Padstow, Cornwall
Typeset in 11pt Bembo by Troubador Publishing Ltd, Leicester, UK

Matador is an imprint of Troubador Publishing Ltd

For all the women who gave me wings –

I did not always realise you were there.

The thistle is the national emblem of Scotland,
defined as both a weed and a flower.
Its prickly beauty symbolises pain, protection, pride
and courage.

pretty rose thistle
you prick
yet you protect
my heart
facing the heat
of the sun
with courage

Tina Cathleen MacNaughton

About the author

Tina divides her time between Crowthorne, Berkshire and her home city, Portsmouth. She is married to Andy, and they have three sons and two grandsons. Tina is a fully qualified and licensed acupuncturist, a writer and a poet. She has a BA in Humanities with Literature (First-Class Honours) from the Open University and an MA in Shakespeare and Theatre from the University of Birmingham. She has written and published two children's narrative poetry books, *When the Elves Rescued Christmas* and *Santa's Still Asleep* (WriteRhymes, 2020 and 2021). Her collection of poetry, *On the Shoulders of Lions*, is published with The Choir Press (2021). She belongs to Portsmouth Writers Hub and regularly takes part in Chichester-based open mic group, Words Out Loud. *Delphy Rose* is Tina's first novel.

www.writerhymespoetry.com
write.rhymes@outlook.com

Standing there

I saw you
Standing there
Dark shades
Fading hair

Eyebrows raised
Curling grin
Same husky voice
Tall, still slim.

And I became a girl again
Up on the stage, the girl who could sing
Filled with hopes, full of dreams
So many ideas, but few means.

I could have stayed
But chose to go
Leaving safety of friends
For a new time and place.
But now those memories flood back
Reminiscent in your smile, your face, your voice.

And it makes me think...
Sometimes we take for granted
Those who cared for us the most
And who were also important to us.

It was autumn when I ran into him again.

Just finished work, not too onerous a day and I was thinking about what to have for dinner.

It had been a sociable weekend and I had willingly put aside cleaning the flat, doing the food shop and the laundry and all the other hundred and one monotonous chores that seemed to fill in my life outside of work.

I was thirty-eight then, still single and, despite worried, even pitying, looks from family, friends and acquaintances, I was content and fulfilled all on my own. I had no real longing to pair up with anyone, just for the sake of being a couple.

And there you were. Just standing there, after all those years.

You didn't say anything at first. Just stood there on the pavement, as if catching sight of me had stopped you in your tracks too. Your eyebrows were raised in recognition, and you greeted me with your curling grin, no words. (Which surprised me as you had always had plenty to say for yourself.) I stood, rooted to the ground, disbelieving that it could be you again. Such a long, long time. I was so very pleased to see you. I stood there and mouthed your name. Then walked straight over to you.

'Well, hello you!'

I felt I was smiling like an idiot, as the words came tumbling out.

'It's Delphy Rose!' *you replied, in that sexy, husky voice you always had.*

I was extremely surprised to see you. I probably should have tried to play it cool too. I never was all that good at hiding my feelings. But you would have known that. I gave you a big hug because I was genuinely quite thrilled. You later said you felt quite taken aback by that hug. It was an enormous hug for a small person, you said, and full of feeling. To me, it was just the kind of hug I would give to an old, once very good, friend, with whom I had been close in the past.

'What are you doing down this way, Ben? I thought you had moved away?'

'Well yes, I did move away, quite a few years ago actually. I've just been down visiting my mum and dad.'

'They're both well then?'

'Yeah good, all things considering. Mum had breast cancer last year, but she came through it pretty well. She's in remission now which is a big relief.'

I could see the fleeting fear and worry in his eyes as he told me this. Ben was always very close to his mum, so I knew how hard just the thought of losing her would be for him.

'Must be. Your poor mum. Lovely lady, I really liked her.'

I remembered Ben's mum always smiling and happy, well dressed, upbeat and very welcoming. My kind of lady.

'Yeah, she liked you too. Always thought you were very friendly and chatty. A nice polite girl, she used to say.'

His blue eyes wrinkled into a smile. A very attractive smile and just as I remembered it. Although he was never one to smile just for the sake of it. You had to earn a smile from Ben.

He looked at me for a moment, as if hesitant. I sensed he wanted to talk more, but I knew that, despite trying to act cool and casual, he had always been quite insecure and shy with women. He was quite naïve really, even a little immature for his age. And there was the small matter of the wedding ring on his finger. You didn't reach your late thirties as a single woman without noting those small details very swiftly.

'Fancy a coffee?' he suggested. 'Unless you have to…'

'Sure, why not? We must have a lot to catch up on.'

Sixteen years could be quite a challenge over a coffee, I thought, as we headed in the direction of a new trendy café I liked. We sat and chatted away solidly for over two hours when he suddenly announced he really must get the next train. As in all the corniest love stories, it was as if we had never been apart. We nattered away quite naturally, and it was good fun, as it always had been between us. Ben had always fancied me. Nothing was ever spoken, mainly because we were both seeing other people, but there had always been a connection between us. He later admitted that he had often wondered where I was and what I was doing in life.

He was surprised that I had come back to our hometown, Cowlington, and I was amazed that he had moved away. He had married a local girl, Jenny, ten years ago (I wouldn't know her, he told me quickly, avoiding my eyes), then moved away with his job a few years later. They had one child, a daughter (not his), Rachael, who was twelve years old. Jenny was a single mum when he started going out with her. He now had his own very successful recruitment company. Another surprise; I thought he would have done something more creative or vocational.

We were still friends when I was backwards and forwards from polytechnic but gradually drifted apart as I came home less and less and stayed on in London for my first teaching post. I came back home to Cowlington, our small hometown near the south coast, two years ago when I got a new job, heading up a newly built Special Needs Unit at our old school, now revamped, refurbished and with a strong interest in creative and performance art. My dream job. My specialist teaching subject was music (of course), and Ben seemed pleased that I had carried on my love of music into my work life. Because in a former life, during my late teen years in the eighties, we had been in a band together. We were called The Thistles. And I was the lead singer and songwriter.

And then music happened

As far as I'm concerned, the eighties were the very best time for music, but I'm prejudiced because that's when I did my growing up.

I was kind of a geeky, uncool, anxious sort of teenager. Not particularly cool or overly popular at school, and probably blossomed in the looks department a bit later in life. I went around in a girl crowd of four and I was the brightest and least carefree of us. Quite shy, lacking in confidence, feeling gawdy with my brace, spots and awkward, funny walk, it took me quite a few years to grow into myself. Once I started studying for my O levels, I grew away from the crowd and became more of a loner.

I spent a lot of time in the comfort and security of my little box bedroom, quite happily devouring French grammar, Victorian novels and dissecting deep and meaningful poetry. I was probably regarded as a bit boring and "keen", but I was kind of OK doing my own thing and not following any sort of crowd. I had a focus. To learn as much as possible, get educated and get out of Cowlington.

Cowlington was fun and I have always loved it, but it was a small town, and I was not a small-town girl. I wanted to fly, do more than I saw my family and friends doing. I was a girl with a thirst for knowledge and adventure, and I had dreams.

I got a part-time job at the local Woolworths when I was fourteen and did quite a bit of babysitting and dog walking, so I had my own money even though I was still at school. I started to hang out with some of the girls at work who were a couple of years older than me. I wasn't old enough to drink but could usually squeeze into local pub gigs with the older girls.

Most Thursday and Saturday nights we were out seeing a band, singer, maybe even a performing poet or two. The most famous local poet was a girl called Poet Penny, a feisty punk girl who wrote horrendously gory, self-consciously offensive poems about STDs, periods and abortions. They weren't for the faint-hearted. I used to hang out with Penny a lot when we were young, and we were very good friends for a while. She's probably married to a banker now, shops in Waitrose and has four kids. Most people settle in the end.

Anyway, once I started going out properly and gigging with my new grown-up mates, everything changed for me. Music came into my life. No more dancing at the church hall disco in my peasant skirt to the latest chart-topping pop music. Times were changing and music got angrier and more social and political. Ska came in on the tail end of Punk and groups like Sham 69, The Specials, The Selecter and The Jam influenced dress, hair, clothes and attitude, so by the time I got to sixth form I felt like a different person. Confident, with a clearer sense of identity and better taste – more sophisticated taste (or so I thought…).

I started listening to John Peel's late-night radio show and got to know bands like Joy Division, New Order, The Damned, The Slits, Siouxsie Sioux, The Stranglers, The Cure, The Bunnymen. The list of all the cool bands at that time was endless. The eighties was such a treasure trove of exciting, mind-blowing music. It still seems like a Golden Age in terms of range and sheer diversity of sound and image. I was discovering all the great alternative bands that resonated with my up-and-down teenage hormones and changing moods. It was fabulous to have that outlet.

Unemployment was still high in the early eighties. If you left school at sixteen in Cowlington, the most you could hope for was a job at the local factory or supermarket. That confirmed my feelings about staying on at school and trying for A levels, and maybe university, with a view to going into vocational work, like teaching. So, I studied hard, got a bunch of good O levels and looked forward to a summer off.

I worked a lot of extra shifts in Woollies that summer. I was covering for holidays and saving a bit for the future. I also wanted to have a good time for a couple of months and intended to go to as many gigs as possible. Maybe even get up to London or Brighton to see The Stranglers. The Damned came to our local town hall that August. I bought a ticket for three quid (oh, those were the days!) right at the last minute and went with a couple of friends who were also going on to sixth form.

Good to make a few new friends, I thought, particularly as my old ones all had steady boyfriends now, were working full-time and not often free. Plus, they were still into the sort of vacuous chart-topping pop music I hated, wore ra-ra skirts and had big, New Romantic-type hair, so we had less and less in common.

Seeing The Damned nearly blew my head away. I did not care much for some of the audience participation (never did understand spitting onto the stage), but I was mesmerised by the sheer energy and vitality of the music. The lead singer, Dave Vanian, toe-heeled around the stage dressed as a fully made-up kind of Gothic vicar and belted out great, iconic tracks like "New Rose", "Neat, Neat, Neat", "Love Song" in his totally individual, deep and haunting voice. It blew my mind away and brought all those Gothic novels totally up to date for me.

I said hi to Ian, a guy I had been seeing on and off all summer. I say *seeing*, we had got off together at a party, had a quick snog after he walked me home and been out for a drink a few times. I didn't really think of him as my boyfriend, but I knew he was quite into me. To be honest, I was a bit wary of getting too involved with anyone romantically at that time. I had already had my first sexual experience and it wasn't really all I thought it would be. I'd had a two-year crush on the boy I gave my virginity away to – I hate the phrase "lost my virginity to", as if it was some kind of mishap and I was a mere victim, so I'll stick with *gave*.

I was curious about sex more than anything else. I wasn't naïve enough to think it would make him like me more. I suppose I thought it might make us closer (it didn't). But I did want to see what all the fuss was about. It was OK, nothing earth-shattering. The relationship was short-lived and didn't end particularly well. He dumped me on Valentine's Day for being too demanding... 'Where's my card?' Which I still don't think was an unreasonable request, looking back. I was a little heartbroken and a lot humiliated, so I made the very sensible decision to concentrate on my studies and steer clear of boys for a while.

Note to self: very wise at sixteen. Note to younger women: concentrate on your studies, or having fun, or just finding yourself. There really is plenty of time for men. And sex and romance are not always what they're cracked up to be. They can play havoc with your long-term plans, so I definitely think it is best to stay focused on what you want to do and find *yourself* before you start getting involved in serious, heavy relationships. The Prince Charming era is most definitely over... if it ever did exist.

Back to The Damned. After the gig, a few of us went for a drink at a late-night, run-down bar called Steve's. And yes, it was run by a guy called Steve funnily enough. Steve's played alternative music and went through a phase of being so uncool that it became cool for a while. It was only after midnight when it started to empty, the lights came up and we noticed a couple of tramps wandering around, drinking dregs from discarded glasses, that the place took on a slightly seedy air. Ian introduced me to Ben for the first time that night. They were friends and both played in a band called The Thistles.

I wrote the songs

I could see Ben liked the look of Ian's new "girlfriend", but I can't say I fancied him at that stage. Ian was stockier, more my physical type and better-looking with nice, light blue eyes. And more importantly, after my first disastrous relationship, Ian was head over heels with me. He phoned me regularly, told me how special I was, how beautiful I was. He made me feel significant without stifling me. We sort of fell into a relationship.

I had told him I did not want to have full sex for a while (due to my earlier experience which I did not share with him), and he accepted this without ever putting any pressure on me. We had plenty of fun anyway and spent many happy hours snogging, cuddling and canoodling in his bedroom, conveniently situated at the far end of his parents' house, whilst listening to all sorts of great music.

Ian introduced me to the Buzzcocks and The Undertones, was a great fan of early Beatles and Wings, and ventured into heavier rock bands like Black Sabbath and ACDC. The latter were never really my thing, but I appreciated his diverse tastes. We had fun together and, if not exactly the love of my life, Ian made me feel very happy when I was with him, and that feeling lasted for about a year and a half or so.

I didn't have much to do with The Thistles at first. It was

an all-male band and there was a strict rule that no girlfriends were allowed in rehearsals. This was because there had been problems with girls hanging around with no interest in the music and who could be disruptive. They tended to chat loudly and pestered the guys for drinks and attention. Not me, of course, I was very into the band and didn't feel the need for that kind of girly, demanding behaviour.

At one point, the band almost broke up when lead singer and frontman Dillon's girlfriend left him for lead guitarist Richie. The guys almost came to blows. Fortunately, Richie's ex-girlfriend then got together with Dill which meant a happy resolution. It was all very rock and roll. After that, the group decided it was best to keep girls and romantic relationships away from rehearsal which was probably a sensible idea.

There were five in the band: frontman Dill, lead guitarist Richie, Ben on bass guitar, Ian on drums and Andy on keyboard. I had been to a couple of their gigs, and they sounded quite good. Only problem was they did not have their own sound. They did a lot of covers and some tracks that sounded almost like other more famous songs. There was a second problem. No one could write songs.

***

Me, Ian and Ben were sat on the floor in Ian's bedroom. No snogging for a change – Ben was there. I was flicking through Ian's vast collection of LPs and overhearing the boys' painful attempts to string a song together.

'I've got the title… "Bust it up!" What do you think? It's all about the strikes and social and political unrest. I've got some really good ideas, but I just can't…'

'Seem to put them into words?' I suggested.

They both looked over. The problem with musicians is they tend to think in terms of sounds and notes, not words. Which is why they employ songwriters. It's quite an art to put them together and not many people can do both.

'Here you go, take a look at these. They're not political or particularly "right now, power to the people", but I think it's better to write about what you know really.'

'These are your poems though, aren't they, not really songs?' said Ben, critical as ever.

'Not much difference. Take them, see if you can fit them to the new tunes you've been playing with. If they work, you can have them, if not, don't worry about it. It's OK, I won't be charging you royalties.' I loved mocking them.

I casually shrugged off any perceived criticism, but sometimes felt that Ben was a little competitive towards me and didn't like it when I came up trumps. But I was a bit of a know-it-all at that age, probably still am, and I guess I could be annoying.

'We'll have to speak to the rest of the group,' said Ben ever serious, looking carefully at Ian.

'Yeah, thanks Delphy.' Ian looked quite proud of his clever, musically involved girlfriend.

A week later there was a big bust-up and Dillon left the band. He said he was sick of it anyway, fed up with playing the same old songs, same old gigs and wanted to move on. I personally think he had his nose put out of joint by my new musical offerings, but that's showbiz for ya. Creative types are often moody, I've found, and can be very highly strung.

And they just could not find a new singer anywhere.

We were in Ian's car going to band rehearsal. I was now permitted to come along, as I could be trusted to sit quietly to the side with a drink and offered quite useful feedback, but only if I was asked. I was singing along to Ian's tape of The Slits. The guys looked at each other.

'Strong voice, Delphy,' said Ben, looking across at Ian who looked proud again.

And so it was that I became the new lead singer of The Thistles. And I also wrote the songs we sang.

Waiting for the girl

Being with you is just like coming home,
Feeling less on the outskirts, complete, less alone
A hand slipped into a soft, warm glove
That's how it feels, our own kind of love.

You look at me and I look back at you
And it's clear we both see right through
You're a part of my past, my here, my now
And perhaps my future too.

There are days when I just yearn and ache for you
When I hear your voice, my day turns to gold from blue
And yes, it's hard when I can't see you for a while
But when I think of you, I just can't help but smile.

You touch me in ways I don't fully understand
I don't need to think as I reach out for your hand
Your kiss suggests that you've been waiting too
Waiting for the girl who makes you feel like you
Waiting for the girl who makes your heart feel light
Waiting for the girl who makes you feel just right
Waiting for her to reach right back to you

Waiting for the girl…
Waiting for the girl…

He whispered softly in my ear. 'I'm in love with you, Delphy Rose. I think I always was.'

We had just made love in my flat for the first time. Things had moved on quite quickly between Ben and I since we bumped into each other in the high street. It started with a coffee and a chat, progressed onto exchanging phone numbers and flirty texts, then lunch and a walk in the park. Then a few meaningful, long phone conversations, which culminated in that wonderful afternoon of kissing, holding onto each other and making love in a way I never had before. It felt natural; it felt innocent; it felt magical. It just felt right.

We probably should have done this years ago, we both agreed. But somehow the timing was always wrong. Ben said he thought Ian and I were much more serious than we were, or as Ian would have liked us to be, and was loyal to his best friend. Ben then started going out with Suzie and they were on and off for a couple of years whilst I was away studying. I did continue to sing with the band for a bit, but it became too difficult to get back during term time, which proved the death knell for me and Ian. The Thistles ended up getting Poet Penny on board to sing in my place.

I made the odd "guest" appearance when I was home for the holidays. But it was never quite the same again, and I felt a bit left out of it all, to be honest. Also, it was awkward after I ended it with Ian. I wanted to stay friends, but it's difficult when one of you has moved on and the other is still pining. I felt it was kinder to leave and let Ian get on with his life and find another girlfriend. He could do without me hanging around as a reminder of what he could no longer have. I felt better about it too and could move on without feeling bad about Ian looking a bit lost every time I saw him.

I meant to stay in contact with Ben, but it never really happened and he, being a typical bloke, did not exactly go overboard on keeping in touch. He had his friendship with Ian to think of as well, I suppose, although they didn't stay in contact for long either. Nothing lasts forever, particularly when we are young and have so many opportunities and so much time ahead of us. One thing I have learnt is that, sadly, we don't always realise the value of what we had until after it has gone.

After meeting Ben again, the next few months passed by in a kind of dream. He was attentive, affectionate and sensitive. He messaged me each morning on his way to work and several times during the day to check I was OK, and so that I knew he was thinking of me and us. He told me how much he regretted that he did not ask me out when we were younger. He had genuinely not wanted to step on Ian's toes, held their friendship dear and thought he was doing the right thing by his friend, and with the band, by keeping things between us close but professional and uncomplicated.

I was quite touched when I realised how much he had thought of me in those early days but had kept it all to himself. He told me he was scared of showing his feelings towards me. He thought he would be rejected, as I always seemed so confident, and he was never sure how seriously I would take him. He also thought I had generally seemed happy enough with Ian. When that relationship ended, it seemed as if I needed to move on from The Thistles and my hometown life. He was probably right.

'I was quite happy going to work, going to the football

and down the pub and playing the odd gig. You always seemed to want so much more, Delphy, and I wasn't sure I could give you what you wanted or even keep up with you.'

Ben had done quite well for himself. A successful businessman, he now lived about an hour away which, as he said, was not too far, yet far enough to be a pain in terms of seeing each other regularly. My teaching job was full on, and I didn't have much spare time during the week. But Ben said he would try to visit his parents more often and "work away from home" more frequently so that we could see more of one another.

There were two problems. One was his job, which was busy and stressful. Like most people who own their own business, he was pretty much obsessed with it. He spent a lot of time on the phone, in the evenings, weekends, holidays and even during our extremely precious time together. Constantly checking for messages and picking up phone calls. I tried hard to be the ever-understanding girlfriend, but it could become tedious after a while. I would selfishly, but understandably, want more of him than I was getting during our snatched and scant time together.

The second problem, and not a minor one at all, was his family. His daughter was not his biological child but the result of a previous relationship his wife had before she met Ben. However, and to his credit, he loved and cared for Rachael as his own and she was obviously a top priority for him, work permitting. We talked carefully and seriously about his marriage before we started sleeping together. I had dated a married man once before, although he hadn't been honest with me, so I had not realised what I was getting into. It ended badly and I vowed never to get into that situation again.

Once I eventually found out he was married, I was too

emotionally enmeshed to tell him to leave. I'm afraid I made do with crumbs for several more months before I picked up my pride and self-esteem and walked away, head held as high as my tears would allow. No, dating married men seemed a good way to stay single. Forever on the fringes, always last, least and occasionally. Never first, foremost and always. I wasn't going down that path again.

But Ben was different. This time it felt different. We had known each other from when we were young, knew the baggage and he was totally upfront about his relationship. His marriage was, in his words, "OK, but not great". Not physical and had not been for some time. His wife had problems with depression but had been massively supportive when he lost his job and started up the business. She had "let herself go a bit" and lacked confidence, but she was "his rock" and he could not envisage leaving her or Rachael. He felt sorry for Jenny, was tied to her "for better or worse", and he would not be able to live with himself if he left and made them both unhappy.

He could not and would not put his own (or our) happiness first. Besides, on a practical note, he could not afford a divorce. Too much money had been ploughed into the business, he said. He said all this right at the start of the relationship when the attraction and connection between the two of us could not be denied.

'I'm sorry, darling, but I just never will. Please don't ever ask me. I couldn't live with myself, and I think I would just start to resent and blame you. I don't want anything to spoil our relationship. Apart from the circumstances, it's so perfect.'

And then he would kiss me, long and slow, sensual kisses that made my head spin with love and passion and I could think of nothing better than just being here, with him, whatever the circumstances and whatever the price. Because there would always be a price to pay in that kind of tainted relationship. And it was probably my own sanity.

Still, I was a bright girl and a strong one and I had never come close to feeling like this with anyone before, so I tried not to think too much about the other side of his life and did my best to live my own life as fully as possible in the long absences. Those empty spaces and grey weeks when I could not see him at all and when I lay there alone and sad, thinking of him, trying not to think of him, thinking of him. It was difficult to know which was more painful at times.

Then, finally, succumbing to dreaming of having him all to myself, if only for a few snatched hours. A few stolen hours of utter bliss.

Keithie's squat

It was the summer of 1982, and I had just finished my first year of sixth form. I didn't do as well as expected in the end-of-year exams, which I put down to stress. I was a tense, emotional teenager, had spent too much time and energy on the band and lost focus a little. I resolved to have a good summer, do plenty of extra shifts at Woollies to pay for my travel expenses to interviews in the autumn term. Plus, I wanted to learn to drive and try to get some sort of small car to cart my belongings to and from uni if (*no, when*) I got in. *Positivity*.

I decided to make the most of singing in The Thistles over the summer, as I would have to tell the others I would not be so readily available once I had gone back to my studies. My exams had to come first. I would also have to start seeing less of Ian. And Ben, who always seemed to be tagging along with us. Not that I minded. Ben was argumentative but funny and interesting, and I did enjoy his company. When he wasn't in a bad mood, he made me laugh.

Mid-July, we had a gig at The Rosewood Rooms on the outskirts of Cowlington. We had clubbed together to buy Ian a new drum kit. His was tiny and not producing much of a sound for the larger venues we were now playing in. Friday evening at six-thirty, we were all piled into Richie's van and on our way to set up and get in a thorough soundcheck before The Pink Skinks, our support band, and Poet Penny turned up. You got good value for your entrance fee at our gigs.

I was not a fan of travelling with the guys, especially after the gig when they had downed a few beers. There was a lot of farting and burping, and it was disgusting with all of us squashed in the van together.

'For fuck's sake, Delphy, you're vile. What you bin eating?'

I stuck two fingers up at the laughing lot of them and pulled my scarf up to my face. I was wearing a great outfit for that gig. A pale blue minidress I had picked up from Cathy's, a little second-hand shop that would probably be called "vintage" these days. I teamed it with a sparkly scarf that I could sort of dangle and play with as I was singing. I had bought it from a jumble sale for twenty pence. My hair was plaited at the sides, pinned up Sylvia Plath-style (or so I believed) and crimped at the front. I was wearing a huge pair of dangly earrings, flesh-coloured fishnet tights with customary rip and a pair of red high heels. Oh, and a fake leather-studded jacket, also picked up from a second-hand shop. I wore clothes well, had grown prettier in the last couple of years, so I knew I looked good on stage. I had a bit of eye make-up on, not too much, and a vivid pink lipstick.

The guys wore jeans and black shirts. They were going for a cool, sort of Joy Division/Stranglers, "not-too-try-hard" image. They looked good, kind of professional even, which made a real change. I usually had to nag them to near death to look half decent.

We had a tight set of some good, catchy songs and a couple that were stand-out. And, of course, a couple extra in case of encore. We were going to do an encore anyway. It would take a rocket to get us off that stage early. We had the material and wanted to use it.

Most of the songs were written by me; a couple were collaborations by Ian and Ben, who were becoming more creative and confident with lyrics now they felt they did not always have to "get political". Also, they didn't have Dillon in the background making sarcastic comments about whatever they came up with.

We still did one or two covers, mainly because they were popular with the audience, who felt they were listening to a "real song" if they could recognise a tune and sing along to lyrics they knew. That night we were doing a cover of a cover, The Strangler's version of "Walk on By" and Siouxsie's "Hong Kong Garden". Quite ambitious for a bunch of kids playing at being rock stars!

It was a cracking night. Great turnout, sold a load of tickets and an encouraging crowd. We even made some money for the kitty which was currently run right down due to the new drum kit purchase. Penny was on form and managed to read a few poems that were *not* about her periods. The guys had a word with her this time and asked her to tone it down a little. They were squeamish, they said. Blokes! Just as well they didn't have to put up with them every month, responded Penny, ever the protester.

The support band was OK, but not too good, so we sounded even better. I was still concerned that we lacked our own sound, but we certainly sounded stronger than we used to. Of course, I put that largely down to my presence and creative input! But I think, in truth, the band pulled together a lot more than it had done in the past and had fewer problems with clashing egos. We talked more and made group decisions, rather than risk falling out over silly things that were not very important. We focused instead on practising and playing, which were important.

I was no longer the only singer in The Thistles. Ben and Ian had quite good voices and sounded better on some of the more robust rock tracks like "Dig Down" and "Walk On, Walk Away". It worked well to mix up the voices a bit, but with hindsight, maybe that was why we never really established our own sound in the way some of the other local bands did.

When we took a break that evening, I spotted Keithie in the audience. I was very fond of him and always pleased to see him when he came and supported us. One of five brothers whose mother had died when they were teenagers. Their dad really struggled to bring them up and they had a few stints in care.

Keithie was great, a big-hearted bloke whom I had known since primary school and always chatted with. He was kind, but tough, due to his upbringing, or lack of, and had stood up for me a few times against bullies at school when I was younger. A rough diamond, I had noticed he was living more and more on the social outskirts since he left school, hanging out with older, dodgy characters.

He was an old friend of my brother Neil, but they had less and less in common since Neil had married and had a little boy. Neil had responsibilities now and not much time nor the money to hang out with old mates from school. They would still have a pint together once in a while if they bumped into each other and Keithie wasn't pissed or stoned. We were never sure what his job was. I guess he was on benefits. He was getting very much into a druggie world and didn't always recognise me when I saw him. He was fine this evening though, and when I saw Ben and Ian chatting with him, I walked over to say hello and to see how he liked our new set.

He thought we were great and could see a real improvement, he said. He teased the others, saying that he thought it was all down to the great new lead singer. They had obviously needed a girl on board to sort them all out, he said. He winked at me, and I smiled back. As I said, I liked Keithie, and even at that stage of his life, we were fans of each other. But I sensed a slightly dangerous, reckless side to him then and so was wary of getting too close. Keithie felt too much like trouble at that time.

'Fancy a party?' He smiled. Richie was driving and had work the next day and so he declined. The rest of us went along. I felt a little apprehensive but, typical me, did not want to feel left out or miss a good time.

The party was at Keithie's new digs, a squat close to The Rosewood Rooms. It was my first and only time in a squat and I was a bit nervous. We could smell weed and Keithie went straight to the smoking circle, sat down and got stuck in. Penny sat down with him and spent the rest of the evening throwing up in the disgusting toilet, with Ben holding her hair back. He was good like that, plus he fancied her like mad like most guys. Ian and I had a few drinks and then moved on.

I said goodbye to Keithie, but he was totally stoned and barely recognised me. I didn't see him for quite a few years when I worked in London after poly, and we lost touch. I often wondered what happened to him and was saddened when I found out that Keithie had become more and more involved in drugs. He ended up doing heroin, became a supplier to pay for his addiction and wound up in prison. Unsurprisingly his story did not end well.

Keithie was put into the same prison as some extremely hardened, dangerous criminals. I was so sorry to learn that shortly after he was released from jail he died of an overdose. Some believed it was not accidental. God knows what happened to him in there. When I heard of his tragic end, I took it as proof that underneath that rough, tough, careless exterior was a vulnerable little boy who lost his mum far too young. Even though I hadn't seen or heard of him for years, I still wept when I heard how his life had turned out. Because, underneath it all, he was a good-hearted, nice guy who didn't have too many chances in life. And in many ways my hero. Poor Keithie. He deserved more from life.

A few weeks after the squat party, my dad showed us the headline story of our local evening newspaper in disgust.

'Look at that load of wasters,' he said. 'Cheek to complain about rights, they want to get off their arses and work for a living.'

The squatters had staged a protest for squatters' rights and made front-page news in the local rag. To be fair, it was a quiet week in Cowlington. I smiled to myself. No need to tell my hard-working dad that I was partying with "that load of wasters" a few weeks earlier. Rock and roll. It all felt quite daring to a rather naïve eighteen-year-old, still studying hard at school, singing in a band and dreaming of a way to get out and make more of her life.

It's snowing

It's coming
Swirling, whirling
Fragile snow petals
Prettily twirling,
Like silent sky dancers
Softly scattering,
Iced bridal confetti.

And together,
Side by side,
Towards a winter's sky,
They sat
They waited
They watched.

Glistening, icy pearls
Falling quietly, gently
Lacing trees, leaves
White lining walls
Slowly filling crevices
Sugar icing rooftops,
A flourish of frozen fairy dust.

It's coming more thickly now
Layering down a white, velvety rug
Enveloping and protecting,
Snuggling the natural world
Transforming fields and meadows
Into a magical, mystical snowscape,
Still, desolate, but oh, so beautiful.

A winter wonderland
An icy lull
Where time is frozen.

And together,
Side by side
They sat
And waited
And watched.
It's here now
Hush.

In those early days I often wondered what you would say if you knew. I felt like talking to you about it, but I had kept it to myself for so long. It was almost as if it had happened to someone else. Another lifetime, someone else's story and not mine to tell at all. I wasn't even sure I could speak the words.

We were sitting in the car together a week before Christmas. It would be the last time we would see each other until after the new year, which was only two or three weeks, but I was dreading Christmas without you. Absolutely dreading it.

It was one of those still, bleak but atmospheric wintry days. The sky was white, filled with the snow that had been predicted to fall over the next few days. It looked as if it was about to come down prematurely. We sat silently, cuddled up close and watched as the first few flakes began to fall gently down. It was so romantic. Bleakly, starkly beautiful. Desolate loveliness.

Ben had taken me to a little village about an hour away for a pub lunch. Our Christmas lunch, I supposed. We had exchanged gifts. I gave him a history book (he still loved history) and a joke mug he could use in his office. I also wrote him a song about us and how we first met all those years ago in the run-up towards Christmas. The festive period was a special time for us and yet we would celebrate it with other people. It felt sad and all wrong, but I did not say anything about my feelings. Ben gave me a CD of a new band he thought I might like and a scarf. We had decided to keep to small, token gifts and I obviously had to be careful with my choices.

I had secretly hoped he might give me something romantic. Not expensive of course, but perhaps a small trinket, some red roses, something personal and intimate. I was a little disappointed with his idea of a scarf that I chose myself. I would have preferred something that expressed his feelings for me, a little something that said *I love you* or *I'll miss you at Christmas*. Something special. But no, nothing like that. I quickly brushed my disappointment aside. They were only gifts and things didn't matter.

I didn't ask what he had bought his wife and I didn't want to know. It was best to blank out the details of his other life.

After lunch we went for a walk, then sat and chatted in the car and talked about anything other than our enforced absence. He always dealt with the gaps better than I did which bothered me quite a bit. Not that I wanted him to be upset, but sometimes I felt that I shouldered the pain and burden of our relationship. He walked away, back to his family, casual and carefree. Or maybe he felt it too but was able to hide it better?

When pressed, he would say he wanted us to last a long time. He reasoned that we had more of a chance if we stayed as calm and relaxed as we could and didn't "ramp things up emotionally", whatever that meant. It made sense, of course, and I admired and envied the apparent ease with which he could do this. I really struggled when we were apart, but then I did not have the family commitments he had, I reminded myself. It was just me when I closed the front door of my lovely, homely, but sometimes very quiet, little flat.

I used to be so happy there.

Not that I would be alone over the holidays and, of course, I did have a certain amount of lesson prep and admin to do. That was teaching for you; it never really ended at three-thirty or the end of term. It was part of the attraction for me. I liked the commitment and vocation of my job, and I enjoyed being a professional with continued responsibilities and duties beyond my working hours.

Christmas Day and Boxing Day would be spent with my parents and my brother Neil and his family. The day after Boxing Day the family were over at Neil's for a party. There would be a large extended family get-together on the Friday between Christmas and New Year, and I had been invited to a New Year's Eve Ball with a group of mates. New Year's Day I would probably have a much-needed sofa day. So not too shabby a festive break. Even so, I would miss Ben tremendously and part of me could not wait to get it all over with, which was a shame as I usually loved Christmas.

I would have to distract myself constantly, so as not to let myself imagine Ben's Christmas with his wife and daughter. A cosy, family Christmas. I wondered how much he would miss me. He said he would be thinking of me. I should hope so too! I never really felt guilty about Jenny or Rachael if I was truthful. It felt as if Jenny had given up and almost did not deserve to have Ben. And Rachael was just a little girl. We both took great care to be respectful and discreet at all times. No holding hands or kissing in public if there was any chance that we could be seen by anyone who knew either of us.

Of course, there was always some level of risk in being seen out together, but we tried not to be reckless and to minimise being found out. We both wanted to continue to see one another and neither of us wanted Jenny and Rachael to be hurt. I did not call Ben without messaging first and I did not send late night or early morning messages. I tried my best to keep him safe and protect him and his family. So yes, it was an illicit relationship which should not have been happening, but rather like honour among thieves, we tried to keep it as clean and decent as possible. No sexting or exchanging erotic photos for us! Which I would hate anyway, so I'm glad sex stayed in the bedroom. The other times we just talked and had a laugh, like any other couple. Probably more than most couples.

It never seemed to be just about the physical for us. Our time together was always limited, so everything was more special, enhanced. We had to make the most of every moment, not usually knowing when the next time would come.

I relegated responsibility to a certain extent. I was single and free so, rightly or wrongly, I felt that Ben's conscience and his feelings about his wife and daughter were his problem, not mine. He had to make his own peace with that, but I would do nothing to push my own agenda or threaten his home and family. He knew he could trust me on this. I was not about to become a psycho bitch.

I knew that Rachael suffered from bad asthma attacks, had been hospitalised three or four times and was always a worry. I gathered that Jenny was typically in a fairly depressed, low mood, suffered from anxiety and was very dependent on Ben. She did not leave the house unless she had to, mainly to drop off or collect Rachael and to do shopping and small errands. He worried that if he left Jenny, the shock and trauma would adversely affect the health of them both.

Another reason for him to stay in a stale, boring marriage then. He liked to think of himself as a man with a certain degree of integrity. A man who tried hard to do the right thing. I hoped I was not too guilty a secret for him to bear, but he seemed good at compartmentalising. Like a lot of men, I guessed.

Although I occasionally asked after his wife and daughter, I generally felt that our kind of relationship worked better if it was not overthought or over-discussed. I did ask him once or twice if he thought she suspected. He said no, he gave her no reason. They had not slept together for several years now. Jenny often slept in Rachael's bedroom if she had breathing difficulties during the night. Mother and daughter were very close.

I wondered if her daughter was a solace for Jenny and whether she indulged Rachael a little too much so that Ben felt left out. I kept this to myself. I had enough experience of the dysfunctional families I encountered as a teacher to have picked up quite a bit of psychology. Their relationship did not sound healthy to me.

Ben always maintained that there was nothing physical between them. He said he could not talk to her as he talked with me and certainly did not have much fun with her. However, she was very supportive in her own way, looked after him and the household impeccably and made very few demands of him.

'She doesn't demand anything from me, just that I am not away on business too often. She likes me back for my dinner each evening, as often as I can, work permitting. And I don't *give* her very much,' he said without feeling. 'A card on Valentine's Day, maybe some flowers if I think of it, a present for her birthday, a few nice gifts at Christmas, the very occasional weekend away and Rachael always comes with us. That's all.'

There was a coldness to him at times that disconcerted me. I almost shivered as I sat next to him and watched the pale, lacy flakes coming down a little faster against the front car window. I looked at his pale skin and tired eyes, worn out from too much work and lacking in fresh air and exercise. He was ageing prematurely, worn down by life already.

He no longer fancied Jenny, finding her physically unattractive.

'She's let herself go, probably my fault, for not giving her enough attention and showing no interest in her physically.'

She did not want to go out, socialise, did not have friends or do very much apart from looking after the house and Rachael. He felt awful and guilty saying it, but he found her boring, irritating and dreaded them getting old together. And yet, he stayed.

'She's the very opposite of you really. I know who I'd prefer to have on my arm. I'm so proud to be with you. We look right together, always did really. I feel alive when I'm with you, Delphy. Half-asleep when I'm with Jenny.'

And still you stayed.

I wondered how his wife really felt inside, knowing her husband did not find her attractive or want a physical relationship with her anymore. Apparently, it was never discussed. She had given up asking for him to take her to bed and had stopped crying about his apparent withdrawal from her. I did wonder what came first, her depression, or the feeling that she was undesired. She must have realised that she was not wholly loved by someone she needed and apparently adored. He was fond of her, yes, but never that hungry, must-have-now love. *She must feel awful*, I thought sadly. But then I felt sorry for Ben too, stuck in a dry marriage and that sterile, claustrophobic home. I wondered how he could keep on pretending.

'When I'm with you, I can be myself. When I go home, my mask goes on,' he told me flatly one day.

Do we all wear masks? Is that how we get by in this life?

He admitted to feeling "a little embarrassed" that Jenny was his wife and was glad she had no interest in going to work events.

'They would look at us and think, why is Ben with that old frump?' he said. Again, no trace of emotion.

But Jenny was kind and caring, a good person. She had a sad childhood and some harsh knocks in life. I did wonder why he had been attracted to her in the first place.

'She wasn't like that then. Quiet, but then she was a single mum with a young child. And I admit I settled. I had my own heart knocked a few times and I was sick of being treated like shit by women I fancied and thought I loved. I should have waited a bit longer, I guess.'

'For me?'

'For you, Delphy Rose.'

We sat side by side.

'Come on, better get back.'

We decided Ben would drop me off at the station, rather than come back to my flat, as there was a risk of getting stuck in traffic if the snow continued and worsened. I could easily jump on a train and would be home in half an hour or so. One last kiss for Christmas, then that would be it for a few weeks. I felt close to tears, said nothing. Like a good girl. I did not want to put any more pressure on Ben.

I wore my own mask.

In some ways he had more to cope with. This explained why he had to be harder and less emotional about us, I told myself. We always make excuses for those we love the most. And they are the ones who have the potential to hurt us more.

So, no more Ben for the most romantic time of the year. A Ben-free Christmas. The price one pays. Feeling a little Bridget Jones-ish, I sat on the train and tried not to dwell on that last quick, careless kiss. Ben seemed in such a rush to get away and did not want to linger. I could have made that kiss last forever. Understandably, given the weather conditions of course, but that feeling that he wanted to get home quickly stung all the same.

I fastened my mask on more tightly.

Well, hello you

Well, hello you, you're back again
Just when I thought I was all settled.

Here you are, slightly disruptive as usual,
Nudging memories, thoughts and feelings
Surfacing emotions I imagined
Were securely and safely stowed away.

Forcing me to rethink, to reassess
And making me curious.
You always did make me sparkle and feel alive
Yet also accepted me at my moody worst.

And you always seem to turn up
At just the wrong time!
What is wrong with you?!

Can't you ever come along
When it's convenient?
I don't know, when we're free,
Unattached and perhaps available?

Still, I have to admit
It's always very nice
When you are around.
Prodding and pricking me
With your sharpness and wit

Making me laugh
But never allowing me
To get away with anything.

Welcome back
And stay this time
I missed you.

I hadn't seen you for a while. I'd had to give the band a miss for a bit as I was revising for mock A levels. I hadn't been at rehearsals and had to forgo the pre-Christmas gig, much to my disappointment. Ian and the others understood, but I knew you were annoyed with me. You showed me less attention than you normally would. I didn't quite understand why at the time, just thought you were being sulky old Ben (you could be very sulky), but I later realised you probably missed me and that's why you were punishing me a little.

Although, and maybe because, I didn't see so much of Ian, we were still very much a couple and enjoyed our time together when we had the chance. Or rather, when I could fit him in between studying. He was very understanding, undemanding and good about it. As I said, ideal boyfriend material. Unfortunately, he didn't set my heart on fire, hence we were not going to last.

It was Christmas Eve. Ian and I were cuddled together, part of a large group in The Old Snug Tavern, one of our favourite pubs, when Ben walked in with Suzie on his arm. I had never seen him with a girlfriend before and I felt a twinge of something. I didn't know what that feeling was at the time, but retrospectively I think I may have felt a bit jealous and put out. Just a little bit. I was used to being *Top Girl*, the only girl in the band and the centre of attention. I sensed Ben still had a soft spot for me.

Not sure why I would feel like this because I never found Ben overly attractive when we were young, and I was having a nice enough time with Ian. In fact, he was surprisingly good in bed. Extremely enthusiastic, energetic and very much taken with me. It was all very nice. What more could a girl want? Except the feelings on my part were never quite as strong. Always so difficult to get that equal balance. It took me such a long time to find it and I thought I never would.

And there was Ben with a new girlfriend. She was pretty, rosy and freckly. A little young, but then I always thought he was emotionally immature. A bit of a mummy's boy really and very indulged at home. Ian and I sat with the rest of The Thistles and the members of another local band, our friendly rivals, Little Black Kitten. For most of us, that evening was probably the best Christmas Eve ever.

Everyone had finished work at lunchtime and we'd had a skinful in the afternoon. We then went back to our various homes for a quick tea, and we were off out again for Round Two.

We were all on sparkling form in the pub and there was a lot of good, clean banter between the two bands. We did quite a lot of singing, initially to the annoyance of the other punters, but by the end of the evening, they were joining in with us. There was a brilliant, buzzing atmosphere.

Ben came in and sat in the centre of us all, snuggled down with Suzie. He was his usual caustic self. Argumentative, full of clever, know-it-all comments, batting the banter back and forth like a professional. He always could hold a room. Cleverly mimicking with impeccable accents and being a smart-arse as usual. I felt both attracted to him and irritated by him. A common thread in our relationship.

I watched you as if for the first time that evening, as I saw you slip your hand into Suzie's.

I brushed aside the little pang of feeling I had and which I did not understand. It seemed strange to see you with a girl and acting so romantically. I found myself thinking what a nice, caring boyfriend you would make. I cuddled up to Ian and drank my cider and ignored that nagging feeling that you and I could be much better suited as a couple.

Two sides of the same coin; that chemistry and battling of wills can be so exciting in a relationship and keep it from going stale. So many relationships seem to dwindle and fizzle out, I've found. And yet I stayed with Ian.

Even at that young age, I sensed Ben was the complicated one in the band. There was something unknowable and complex about him which could be high maintenance, I thought. He noticed and questioned just about everything. And he had something to say about everyone too. Always provoking, always on the lookout for an argument, that was Ben. Stimulating, but also annoying.

Whereas Ian was the very opposite. Cheerful, laid-back, obliging. Had his own ideas and opinions of course but rarely felt strongly enough to argue his corner. Ian was one of the good guys and thought the absolute world of me. That was all I wanted at that time, nothing more. Maybe I was wearing a mask even then?

Sleeping, dreaming, waking

Drifting off to sleep
And thinking of you
Wishing you were here
Lying with me too.
Reliant on memories,
Held tight in your arms
Captivated again by your
Still boyish charms.

Recollecting your smile
Gentle voice, slender hips.
Soft whiskers, sensual kisses
Your soft, tender lips.
Wishing I could lose myself
Disappear, dissolve
Consumed by your kiss
I wish, I wish, oh how I do wish…

Dreaming, always dreaming
Still dreaming of you
Kind of drawn in
Or so it seems.
Wonder what dreaming of you

Really means?
That you're locked in my heart?
Perhaps you were there from the start.

Because you're my special one
My sun, my stars, my moon
Whom I cherish and adore,
But always leave needing more.
When I'm with you, my love,
It's heaven, such bliss
But when we're apart
There is so much to miss.

Waking, again waking
Again, I think of you
Wondering how you are
Are you still OK too?
Praying you stay safe
And have a good day.
Willing you stay strong,
Because this cannot be wrong.

Hoping you're respected,
Well regarded, treated just right.
Because you're precious, you're lovely
My sweet, gentle guy
What we have is oh-so special
I will never say goodbye.

And so began a new year of waiting, longing and trying to steal as much time for us as we could. Your work became increasingly demanding. Rachael had a very bad asthma attack in January which brought things to a halt between us, yet again, during those spring months.

Sleeping, dreaming, waking to another day without you. It felt physically painful at times, the longing. You seemed to be OK though.

Busy, distracted, detached even. The calls became less frequent.

"Be strong, hold on a bit longer, just let me get this job out of the way and I'll be all yours again", you messaged.

All mine? It didn't feel like it.

You're still here

You're inside me
Growing within me
Tiny, tiniest speck

Gnawing at me
That ache of anxiety
As I wake each day

I feel no different really
No sickness, thank God
But then I realise with a thud
In my heart, in my gut,
You're still there.

The dark little secret.

Knowing I am different
From the other girls
Suddenly a grown woman
Old enough to be a mother
But still feeling like a kid myself.

Scary, bewildering
Going to bed praying, hoping
For an un-miracle
But next day, you're still there.
I feel no different

But I am different
I have you now.
But I can't have you.

Penny was pregnant. In the club. Up the duff. In the family way. There was no good way of saying it. I heard her being sick in the toilets during a gig at The Railworkers Inn. And yes, it was next to a railway. I was surprised when I heard Penny throwing up. She normally had a cast-iron constitution for alcohol and could drink most of us under the table. She emerged from the cubicle looking vaguely green, dark shadows under her eyes, looking decidedly worse for wear.

'You OK, Pen?' She looked anything but OK.

She burst into tears. Big, blobby tears rolling down her cheeks. I'd never seen her like that and felt shocked. She told me she had been seeing a bloke "on and off" for about six months. He was using her, I surmised, but kept that to myself. She was head over heels with him. He said he loved her too. There was only one problem in this perfect arrangement – he was already married and had three kids.

He wanted her to have an abortion (of course he did, I loved this guy so much already!) and offered to pay the total cost. Oh, the romance, the chivalry! The complete arsehole.

'Is that what you want?' I asked tentatively.

I knew what I would have done, but I wanted to make sure she had made her own mind up and realised she had choices. She did not have to fit in with Thirty-Five-Year-Old Married Guy's convenient (for him) get-out plans. I had not liked the sound of him from day one. The M word was sufficient for me. Married.

I was so much more sensible when I was younger. Or maybe life was simpler? Or do we just make it more complicated as we grow older? Perhaps there are good reasons not to break the rules in life. Maybe all the moral codes and religious instructions are in place to protect our hearts and save us from agony, apart from, well, living good lives.

Penny was obsessed with Married Guy, however, and could not be told.

She was booked into a private clinic in the neighbouring city on Wednesday. Her dad and gran knew nothing. She had confided in her older sister, Gillian, who was taking half a day off and driving her to the clinic. Gillian was supportive, discreet and matter of fact. Just what you wanted in an older sister. I offered to go with them, and Penny squeaked a tearful, 'Yes please.'

I refrained from asking why Married Guy was not taking her. Probably picking up his kids from school, I guessed. And doing all he could to blank the image of the teenage girl he had been sleeping with, having a very adult procedure to get rid of the tiny human being they had both created inside of her. Or maybe he was buying his wife yet another bunch of flowers to ease his guilt a little? Or even already onto the next vulnerable young girl who wanted a bit of love and attention? I was so much more savvy, black and white, even a tad cynical about relationships when I was a young girl. Very few grey areas for me then. More sensible in some ways than in later years. Or does everything become hazier and *less certain* as we age?

I felt sorry for Penny on the journey down. Her sister chatted away casually about nothing and everything, trying to keep things real. Penny and I sat in the back listening to music. Poor Penny, all those clever poems about teenage pregnancy, abortion and relationship tough talking. She must have felt as if she was living out one of her musings on teenage angst and trauma. Smart Penny, she never would have envisaged herself in this situation. She sat quietly, tears close to the surface, trying her best to seem strong but looking as fragile as I had ever seen her.

The staff at the clinic were all lovely, friendly, reassuring. There was no judgement, no funny looks, no *you young girls will never learn* kind of attitude. It was not as clinical as I imagined. Nothing like a hospital, family planning clinic, nor doctor's surgery. The clinic was almost warm and welcoming and decorated in soft colours. There were fresh flowers, soft comfy chairs and nice new magazines in the waiting room. If only we were there for another reason, we might have enjoyed a sit down and a quiet browse through *Women's Monthly*. Maybe not.

The pleasant motherly lady on reception could have been anyone's mum, with her beaming smile and soothing voice. She was Northern, I noted, and called Penny her *little pet*. Little touches, tiny human gestures. They make such a difference in traumatic situations.

I sat next to Penny whilst her sister went to park the car.

'I need the loo,' sniffed Penny, looking as if she was barely holding it together.

My heart went out to her.

'If they call, do you want me to go in for you?' I quipped, trying to keep things light.

Penny rolled her eyes and disappeared down the corridor. I picked up a magazine and tried to silently rip out an article about a band I liked. The receptionist looked up and just smiled and carried on with her typing. I thought it was important that I stayed calm for Penny. I was there for her, that's all she needed from me. A reassuring, supportive presence, someone to sit beside her, talk to and cry with, if necessary. She needed a good friend.

Penny was gone for a while, and I started to wonder whether she had changed her mind. Maybe she decided to go ahead, have a baby, give up her dreams of university and live at home, or even get a council place. I imagined her future reduced to trying to cope alone with a tiny, crying baby. Sitting there in a grotty little flat, holding a fractious baby and crying herself, mourning the loss of Married Guy.

He would obviously ditch her when he was fed up with playing second happy families. An even worse scenario would be Penny sitting in the grotty flat waiting desperately for his occasional visits. Perhaps he would turn up occasionally out of guilt, pity or boredom with his wife and "real" family.

Penny shone and sparkled; she deserved so much more.

I'm going to write a song about him, I thought. I did and called it "Because You Know I'm Worth It". It became one of our most popular songs, so something positive did come out of the experience. Penny and I always exchanged a little smile as I sang it. The best songs generally have a real story behind them, often painful. Belting them out eases that pain. Penny said singing "Because You Know I'm Worth It" in the shower helped her through. *You're welcome.*

Penny eventually emerged from the toilet, looking very different. She looked happy, relieved and was smiling through her tear-stained face.

'I've just come on,' she mouthed at me.

'You're joking?' I asked in disbelief. As if this was the time for jokes.

She shook her head. Talk about timing. Just a little bleed and it was a very different day. But that's a story most women know at some point in their lives. We both started to laugh, sort of hysterically really. Penny's sister walked in at that point and just looked at us hugging, laughing and crying together.

'You are fucking joking me!' she said, right out loud in the waiting room.

The receptionist shot her a warning look. No swearing in the abortion clinic. Obviously. They were very good about it all. Penny never did have that abortion. Her timing, like her poetry, was impeccable. The kind Northern lady on reception looked so pleased.

I wouldn't have thought she got a lot of job satisfaction in her line of work, and she must have tried hard to stay jolly in that environment. How awful to have to sit and watch women walking in weeping and then stumbling out crying even harder. But someone had to do the job and she did it with a good heart and kindness. Bless her, she remembered or understood what it was like to be young, hurt and lost. Kind hearts make all the difference in difficult times, and hers was golden.

When we got back into the car, I was surprised to see that Penny's dead hard sister had tears in her beady brown eyes. She rubbed them away quickly. Then she made Penny call up Married Guy from the phone box across the road. If she didn't ditch him, she said, she would tell their gran and dad what had happened. Gillian did not mess around, so Penny obeyed.

We all stood together in the phone box whilst Gillian made Penny tell him to sod off and leave her alone. The party was over as far as he was concerned. Then Gillian grabbed the phone and told him, in no uncertain terms, that if he ever contacted Penny again, she would tell his wife and employer. I'm not sure what his employer had to do with it, but I think Gillian just called on all the authority she could think of.

'And next time, pick on someone your own age to have sex with or you'll be getting a call from the boys in blue.'

'She's legal,' he protested.

'I don't care. Our mum died last year and she's vulnerable, so we could get you for taking advantage of her, sexual harassment and grooming of an emotionally fragile young woman.'

Again, Gillian seemed to be making it up as she went along, but she sounded authoritative and scary.

'And you're married. And you should be ashamed of yourself. Stay away or I'll be calling your wife next.' That did it. Married Guy was audibly reduced to a feeble, pathetic wreck. Gillian slammed the phone down, leaving him on uncertain ground. She was on fire. And I felt proud of her. An early example of woman power in my life.

'Now then, girls. First, Penny, you are to promise me that you will never, ever shag a married man again, or even date or snog or have anything at all to do with a married man in your entire life. Unless it's your own husband of course. Do you understand me?'

Penny nodded nervously. Gillian could be terrifying once she got going.

'Because it never ends well, you listen to me. You'll always come second or even third after his wife and kids, then his job. You'll get the crumbs; you'll be last and least; and it will end painfully, as it always does, trust me. And it's beneath you. Look at you, gorgeous, bright, funny, you deserve so much more than a monthly shag and a sexy phone call when it suits him.'

'It wasn't like that though,' protested Penny, still not quite believing that the object of her passion and obsession was, in fact, a total shit.

'It's always like that. I had an affair with one of my teachers when I was fifteen. Bald guy, always moaning, could barely get a hard-on. Don't know what I saw in him. Thank God I had the sense to go on the pill, at least I didn't get pregnant. And whilst we're on the subject, that's where you're going next week with me, the Family Planning Clinic. So, no more married men and we'll sort out proper contraception, OK?'

We were both speechless... Gillian and one of our teachers? At fifteen? But that was all she would say on the subject. As I said, she was a tough cookie. Not sure whether the sexual harassment allegation would have held up in court, but she sounded convincing and obviously put the wind up Married Guy.

A couple of weeks later, we went into town and spent the two hundred quid that Married Guy had given Penny for the abortion. Blood money, Gillian called it. May as well get something good out of him. Penny bought herself a new pair of shoes and a dress; we each bought a new LP; and then she treated us to a lovely meal at the new French restaurant, Le Petit Pois. No one would ever call an English restaurant The Little Pea, but it sounded good in French.

Penny would never write another poem about abortion. It was no laughing matter, she said.

In fact, she became a much more responsible, serious, and better writer after that. She did write one more hilarious comedy poem though. "Thirty-Five-Year-Old Married Twat" always received a good laugh. Pain breeds learning and sometimes creativity too. And being able to laugh again helps us to navigate through pain.

Penny survived, moved on and grew up. I wish I had remembered her sister's wise words later in life. Married men... it's always like that. You get what's left. You get the crumbs.

Lovely summer

We sit quietly
By the riverside
Listen to leaves rustle
Feel the sun's warmth
Caress our skin
Listen to birdsong as
Summer blossoms waft
On the slight breeze of
Soft, subtle fragrance.

We sit together
Side by side
It's just us.

That first summer together was blissful. I think of it as our summer; it seemed to belong to us. It was just for us. When we saw each other, happily and frequently then, we walked for miles and miles, my hand in yours, talking, smiling, laughing. The sun seemed to shine throughout those summer months. It felt as if we could never get enough of each other.

'Get a room, you two,' someone called out, as we kissed and embraced on a quiet street corner.

You blushed; I giggled. We were like a pair of school kids really. Back to how we were in our younger days, or how it should have been. We were trying to recapture the past and I think we both knew it. But it all felt so right. We were in our own little bubble, as we walked along together. It was easy to forget other people, other responsibilities, our other lives. I was lucky being a teacher; I practically had the whole summer off. A little preparation for the year ahead, but I had been teaching for quite a few years by then, so I more or less had the job under my belt.

When things were this good, I wondered if I should talk to you about what had happened that night all those years ago. I wondered if you knew anything about it, although I doubted that.

And I did not want our precious bubble to burst, so I held back.

I enjoyed my work. Loved helping the kids to reach their true potential. For most of them, their achievements were tiny by more able-bodied standards, but small steps meant so much to them. It was wonderful to watch the children grow in confidence and ability. It was so important for them to absorb themselves, forget their individual pain, anxieties and limitations and feel free for a short while. It was immensely rewarding watching the children engaged and happily lost in an absorbing, enjoyable activity.

It was how I used to feel with you at the start. You were an escape, a guilty secret, a fantasy lived out. I could spend ages looking out of the window, staring into the distance and thinking of you and our time together. Wondering what you were doing, who you were with, how things really were at home.

Did you kiss your wife on her mouth? Did you linger? I never asked. I presumed not and preferred not to know. I did not want to risk you feeling you had to lie to save my hurt feelings. It was much better not to know too much. Did you all cuddle on the sofa together watching TV, in a cosy family huddle whilst I sat in my flat on my own? Marking papers, cleaning up, reading, watching TV, listening to music. I could keep busy. I could work hard at trying to distract myself from thinking of you too much.

I often wondered if I should get another man. You couldn't blame me, could you? All that time on my own, all those gaps and absences whilst you were with your wife and daughter. But I knew I could not. I'm a one-man woman, I've learnt. Once in love, really in love, I'm hooked; no one else will do. A one-trick pony. No one could match how you made me feel and I did not want them to.

We met for lunch one afternoon in July. The pub by the river, our usual place. Out of the way, where we thought we would be very unlucky if we were spotted by anyone either of us knew. We each had a ploughman's lunch, and I had a small glass of white wine. As usual, Ben had to pick up his daughter a little later, so he wasn't drinking and was clock-watching to a certain extent. I tried not to mind. We walked along the river afterwards, arm in arm, found a shady spot and sat down to hug and kiss.

'I won't be able to see you for a while, Delphy,' he said quietly. We rarely addressed each other by our names – it was generally just the two of us together and there was no need. I loved the sound of my name floating on his voice. But my throat felt suddenly constrained on hearing those dreaded words.

'Why is that, Ben?' I replied, my heart jolting to a stop, my mouth feeling numb with anxiety.

I'm addicted to you, I thought as the butterflies lurched in my tummy. *I must be addicted. I really should not feel ill at the very thought of not seeing you.*

'Don't worry, it will be OK.'

He placed his hand carefully on my arm. I hated it when he did that. He was not a naturally tactile, physical person. This felt like a calculated attempt at trying to be something he was not. I felt managed. I felt I was being coerced, handled. Like a needy little girl who could not cope without him. The gentle physical gesture had the opposite effect of reassuring me. It made me want him and need him more, and I resented him for making me feel like this.

'It's just work, that's all. I'm coming to the end of one of my biggest contracts, and I need to make sure I get more business in by the end of the year. It will be fine, and I will come through this, but I need you to be there for me and to be strong for me.'

I hugged him and wondered how long it would be this time. We needed to speak more frequently on the phone though, I urged. Messaging, even daily, was not enough for me. I liked to hear his voice, catch up properly. Not every day, of course, I didn't need that. Just a good chat once a week and maybe a quick catch-up at another point in the week if he had time.

He wasn't very good at calling me and one of my main complaints (I did not think I had many) was that we did not talk very often during the protracted gaps and absences.

Ben seemed to be more comfortable with these silent times than I was, and I resented him for that. Surely, he should miss me as much as I missed him? But I guessed he had his own business, his family responsibilities and generally more on his plate than I did to keep him occupied. *And he was married.* That small voice I tried so hard to squash came to the forefront again.

He's married to another woman, and he will never leave her for you. He says he loves you, but he must love her more. Otherwise, why would he stay?

But I knew it was more complicated than that. More difficult. That was one of his favourite words. *Difficult.* 'I'm sorry the traffic was bad, I'm home now, I can't call you now, it's difficult.' 'She's back home now, I can't go out again, she'll think it's odd, it might be difficult, I'm sorry.' 'No, I never go out at that time, I'll call you after the weekend. It's difficult right now.'

Always, always so *difficult*.

'But hey, you know I'm worth it,' he said with his cheeky, boyish grin that made me think of him as a nineteen-year-old again. And made my heart melt a little more for him.

Then a sudden, unwanted jolt from the past, as his words also reminded me of the song I wrote when I was eighteen, "Because You Know I'm Worth It". The song inspired by Penny's Married Waste-Of-Space Guy. I felt distinctly uncomfortable.

I said little, as I did not want to make him unhappy, or spoil our time together. That's how these tainted relationships roll. They last because they are not real; time is so constrained and so limited that you dare not say or do anything to make it less than perfect or special. You are constantly on your best behaviour, putting up your best self, never wanting to shatter the mirror, the illusion that together you are ever anything less than perfect. Indestructible, nothing will break you. You are under far more pressures than a normal relationship in some ways. You must feel that you are meant to be together. Yes, the timing and the circumstances may be all wrong, but you will make the very best of what you have. Otherwise, why risk an extramarital, secret relationship that could destroy everything else in your life if you are found out?

My heart was in my mouth as I kissed Ben goodbye. This could be our last kiss for several weeks, or even a few months. But I said nothing and headed for the train back to Cowlington. Ben would never have known the empty hole within me as I sat on that train, already missing him.

Surrounded by so many people, yet feeling alone, lost and wondering how I had come to this point in my life. I had to work hard to adjust my mask that day.

Posters on walls

Ian, Ben and I were out and about promoting the band. We had a potentially huge gig on at The Cornerhouse with three other bands, Little Black Kitten, Hawk Spirit and The Inconsequentials.

It was mid-January, about nine o'clock at night and bloody freezing. Ian had a roll of band posters. Ben carried a small bucket of wallpaper paste and a wide brush. I held a poster up, whilst Ben slapped on some paste, and we glued as many posters as we could around the town. Ian was our lookout. We had been out for a couple of hours and covered quite a bit of ground in our corner of Cowlington. But our fingers felt like icicles, and we were feeling fed up.

'Shall we make this the last one?' suggested Ben, who had clearly had more than enough.

'And what are you three up to then?'

Shit. Two local bobbies. Ian was not much of a lookout.

'Erm, community duties, sir. Getting rid of some old tatty posters to make the community a better place, sir,' Ben spluttered. He was always good at thinking on his feet.

'You're taking them down, are you? So why do you have a bucket of paste and a brush with you at this time of night?'

His observation skills were certainly spot on. Ben had tried and failed to hide the bucket under the back of his coat.

'Erm… it's for charity, sir.'

'Charity, eh?' One of the coppers was the dad of someone at school, so we knew we probably wouldn't be treated too harshly.

'Take it down and we'll say no more about it,' he said reasonably.

Ben started to unpeel the poster which unfortunately revealed yet another of The Thistles posters, promoting our last gig at The Rosewood Rooms. He glanced sheepishly at the officer. Ian and I tried hard not to laugh.

'Go on, get out of here, the lot of you. And don't let me find you pulling this sort of stunt again, mucking up other people's walls. Who do you think you are, bloody Brotherhood of Man?'

We scarpered and popped into the Oak Lodge Inn for a quick pint, half for me.

'Brotherhood of Man?! I wouldn't mind,' moaned Ben. 'But he could have compared us to some cool post-punk band like Echo and the Bunnymen or The Clash or The Stranglers… fucking Brotherhood of Man!' Very Ben. Always the music purist.

You know I'm worth it

We'll be fine, he says
We want to make it work.
I'm busy, work is work
No time for anything else
But that will change
I will come out of this
I have responsibilities
I'm sorry, traffic bad
Can we talk tomorrow?
I forgot I had an appointment
I was late for my tea
Sorry, it got late
I had a long meeting
I had a complaint to deal with
I had a long phone call
(But not with you)
I had to get my hair cut
The meeting ran over
Can we chat next week instead?
I can't just leave the house like that
I'm busy today
I'm married, but not married
They're both at home today

Things will change, hang on in there
I can't talk, she's at home all day
Can you be patient with me?
Can you bear with me a while longer?
Can you wait a little longer?
I want you to do something for me
Can you put your life on hold for me?
Please?
I'll have more time next week
(Grins)
You know I'm worth it.

It had been a month since the day by the river and we had not spoken for more than a fortnight. Several messages each day of course, "Hello sweetie, how are you?", "Good morning, darling, are you OK?", "Thinking of you", "Missing you", "Nighty night", "I do love you". Yes, those were from me. His were less personal, merely informing me where he was and what he was doing. Some days just a "Good morning" and a "Hey, I'm home. Too tired for anything, sorry just been snoozing on sofa all evening. Mental busy, sorry" or a "Morning, just a warning that I won't be in contact much today, sorry".

Sometimes he didn't ask how my day went or how I was for a whole week; he was always so busy and preoccupied with everything else in his life. I tried hard not to notice, but I couldn't help feeling he was moving further and further away from me with each message. How I envied those lovers who spoke on the phone each day, met up for drinks every evening, spent the whole weekend together, just the two of them. Lovely, long lie-ins; sleepy, lazy sex; lying entwined on the sofa with the Sunday papers; unrestricted time just being together as part of a proper, committed couple.

I tried to tell Ben how I felt so that resentment did not set in on my part. But even if he did not say much, I could sense his annoyance at my perceived criticism. He told me he liked nice, kind, caring Delphy. He told me he wanted me to be strong. I began to think he only wanted one-dimensional, easy-to-be-with Delphy. Unfortunately, Ben's distance, his inattention and lack of affection was turning me into a weaker, less attractive and less substantial version of myself. I was becoming less patient with all the excuses and fed up with fitting in around him, his work and family.

I disliked who and what I was becoming but seemed completely powerless to backtrack. I was losing myself in my love, my need, my obsession for Ben and for us. I could feel I was pushing Ben away, making myself less desirable to him, but I had to voice my dissatisfaction and anger that he could be so very lacking. Particularly after all that initial enthusiasm and strength of feeling that he had shown at the very beginning of our relationship. It felt as though I was getting the rough end of the deal and I could not, and would not, be silent.

Obviously, phone calls are limited when a guy is married. Time is limited. He is generally either at work or at home, so I looked forward to Ben working away, even though he was geographically further away from me. If I could not see Ben, then at least we could have a chat from his hotel room, or so I thought. But it never seemed to work out like that. He always had to rush off to some meeting or other, have a drink with someone, follow up on a lead. It could lead to something important, he said, and maintained that, if you ran your own business, you never missed an opportunity to sell or develop.

'It's not like a normal job -- it's my business; it's a lifestyle. Work is work.'

It was Ben's mantra and I heard it many times. The chains of the self-made man.

'We're worth it.' Another of your mantras. Are we? Are you? Doubt was slowly seeping in, and it was starting to rot our relationship and my feelings for you.

Picnic

Lying in a field
Amongst the daisies
Amongst the buttercups
I blow a fairy dandelion
And make a heartfelt wish.

I wish I could go back
And make another daisy chain
That simple connection
So true, so pure
A little daisy chain of love

Our sweet connection to the past
Our sweet connection to our souls.

Whilst Ian and I had moved quite easily into becoming a
steady couple, Ben and Suzie always seemed to be arguing
and falling out over something. Suzie was a few years
younger than Ben and very childish for her age. Well, she
was not more than a child really. Ben seemed to constantly
piss her off for one reason or another, and she frequently
flounced off out of the pub or gig before the end of the
evening.

Then Ben would go outside and try to placate her, and they would head off together. On a couple of occasions, he gave up and came back into the pub or went home alone. I never knew what they found to argue about, to be honest. We would be in the middle of a nice evening out, chatting and laughing, when Ben and Suzie would start talking quietly together. Suddenly, it became heated and angry, and there would be an uneasy atmosphere obvious to us all. One of them would flounce out and the evening was spoilt.

I used to find them quite annoying but always felt a bit sorry for Ben, unsure of what he could have done. He could be a pain in the arse, but I also found him to be kind, caring and supportive. I found myself watching him and Suzie together, just occasionally, and thinking what a nice boyfriend he could be. He seemed more gentlemanly and sensitive than Ian in some ways, and generally better company and more entertaining in others.

It was a warm, spring day during the Easter holidays and all the band members, plus a few extras, decided to take the train into the countryside for a picnic and country-pubbing trip. I was looking forward to a day out and away from revision. Ian and I were taking our bikes and he came to call for me straight after breakfast for an early start. We had not seen much of each other, due to my impending A levels, so days like this had become few and far between for us.

I wore my new bright pink pedal pushers, a white lacey broderie anglaise blouse from Cathy's, a pair of pale pink pumps, a high swishing ponytail tied in a white ribbon and my signature dangly earrings. It was going to be a lovely day, outdoors in the fresh air and sunshine, instead of being cooped up with my books. I loved my studies and always enjoyed learning, but it was good to get away from it all occasionally, particularly on warm, sunny days. I was looking forward to a day of freedom and fun with Ian and our friends.

Ian's face lit up as I opened the door, and he gave me his usual big wet kiss. He reminded me of a very loving, but sometimes slightly overwhelming, affectionate puppy dog.

'You look very nice,' he said. His light blue eyes crinkled cutely into a smile. He was always so obviously pleased to see me and so generous with his love and attention. I came to miss that in years to come. I did not appreciate how infrequently that totally all-accepting and unconditional love comes along in life. Unfortunately, it's the unrequited love that often hits the hardest, makes heads spin and hearts crack and break. It is easy to forget the value of quiet, less passionate, gentle love which creates less drama but is not without significance.

We rode our bikes for a good couple of hours before we joined the others when they hopped off the train. We thought we would probably take the train back with them, especially if we had a few beers. It was a beautiful day, sun shining, all of us in summer clothes for the first time. Ian and I locked our bikes up outside the nearest pub, and we all went walking to the top of the hill and picnicked. The view was glorious, and we sat happily in our large group, relaxed, chatting pleasantly and laughing. Very soon, Ben and Suzie started bickering again. I tried to ignore it, but they were getting on my nerves. I had looked forward to my day out so much and there they were again, picking bits out of each other.

'Oh, shut up, you two! Can you please stop rowing all the time? It's a lovely day and you're going to spoil it again!'

'Well, what's it got to do with you anyway, Delphy? Keep your nose out of other people's business – you're always bloody interfering in someone else's affairs. You shut your big gob up for a change – always telling everyone else what to do!'

Dillon. He had tagged along with his latest girlfriend Becky, Suzie's cousin. Dillon was still bristling after falling out with the band and leaving his position as frontman. He had never liked me, *not sure why*... and was probably even more infuriated when I took over as lead singer. Geeky little Delphy taking over from cool Dillon and even writing half-decent songs! Outrage! I think I was probably a bit too outspoken for him and a smart-arse. He liked his women quiet, malleable and easily impressed. And that was not me.

Dillon was so quick to pounce on me, and so aggressive in his response, that I was initially stunned into silence. I didn't expect Ian to stand up for me, of course. He was not exactly confrontational and always went quiet and looked uncomfortable when there was a disagreement at a band meeting, or any trouble when we were out.

Although I did not need a minder, I must admit I found him to be a bit of a coward at times. Like the time a big, beefy guy knocked into me in a pub and spilt a drink all over my dress. I protested loudly, 'Oi, thanks a lot, mate!' in my typically spontaneous, outspoken way.

Ian turned away and seemed to be doing his upmost to pretend that he wasn't with me.

The beefy guy did not seem to notice Ian and apologised immediately. He asked what I was having, bought me another drink and offered to pay for my dress to be dry-cleaned. Respect. Difficult situation for a boyfriend of course, especially a quiet, gentle one like Ian.

But I have to say his reaction was not unnoticed by me. I came to realise that when the chips were down and a stressful situation occurred, Ian was not your man. The start of me moving away from him, I think. One of those little moments that change perception and feelings and sway the course of a relationship either way.

Back to Dillon. He was always a troublemaker and could get aggressive when he was in the wrong mood or had a few drinks inside him. I gathered myself, fronted Dillon and told him that I was entitled to my opinion. I reminded him that he was no longer part of our band and had no right to be here with us. As far as I understood, he had not been invited.

Dillon started to get nasty towards me. He was red-faced, dark-eyed and wild, swearing and yelling in my face. His behaviour shocked me and took me aback. It was so out of the blue and over nothing to do with him anyway. I had never realised he disliked me so much and it upset me. Of course, I was not going to let that show.

'Steady on, calm down a bit, Dillon. Leave Delphy alone.' It was Richie, lead guitarist. The only one to stand up for me against bully Dillon.

Dillon turned his anger towards Richie and looked as if he was about to punch him. Thankfully, Becky quickly pulled him away and mouthed a pained "sorry" to me. Suzie flounced off down the hill and Ben followed her. *Great day this has turned out to be,* I thought.

I was never happy about the group rule of banning other girls from the band meet-ups. As a girl, it felt a bit weird and disloyal towards my "tribe". However, every single time Suzie turned up, Ben behaved oddly, childish, defensive, as if he was on edge. Their relationship seemed to consist of constantly upsetting each other, breaking up and getting back together again. It was exhausting even to watch.

When everything had calmed down, Ian and I decided

to go off for a walk together. We finally ended up back at the pub.

We went into the garden to find Ben and Suzie having a drink. And another row. For goodness' sake! Suzie stormed off again and Ben followed her again. We could hear a lot of shouting and crying from Suzie. I had never heard Ben shout like that before and it surprised and unsettled me.

I sat with Ian for a bit and then it went quiet, so we wandered out to see if Ben was OK. Suzie had broken up with him again and had gone to find Becky to take the train home together. Ben was standing on his own having a fag and looking really upset.

'Are you alright, Ben?' I asked.

'Yeah, I'll be OK. Look, I've had enough. I'm getting the train back now.'

'Don't go like this – come and have a drink with us.' Ian, kind as ever.

'No, not in the mood, mate. See ya. Bye, Delphy.'

Ben turned away and started walking away from us. He looked sad and dejected and I felt sorry for him. I moved towards him, but Ian stopped me.

'No, leave it, Delphy. He'll be OK. He's always like that when he's upset. He just needs to be alone.'

I used to wonder why Suzie was so unhappy with Ben. He could be so sweet and sensitive and seemed like ideal boyfriend material. Why was she so often upset? Was it all down to Suzie, her bad moods and immaturity? Now I wonder, what was it that Ben said or did or, perhaps more significantly, did *not* say or do that annoyed Suzie so much?

Was there another side to Ben even then? A side I did not see all those years ago?

Love or let me go

Love me like you mean it
Love me with your heart
Show me that you care
Or let me go.

Kiss me generously
Hold me like you must
Make love like you mean it
Or let me go.

Let me in and trust me
Talk with me and share
Tell me that you care
Or let me go.

It may not be forever
May not be your true love
But let me know it matters
Or you have to…
You have to…
Let me go.

Jordan was causing chaos in the classroom again. I did not know what was going on with him that day. He was a pain in the butt most of the time, but especially on days like this. Shouting, swearing, insulting the staff and other kids. Poor little scraps, they had enough to deal with.

Jordan. Eleven years old. Dad in and out of prison, mum hardly able to function, even on a good day. Depressed, no money. Trying to bring up a handful of kids, products of relationships with the various unreliable men with whom she had been involved. They had all let her down somewhere along the line.

Jordan was on the autistic spectrum, had ADHD, anxiety, anger issues and GKWE. God Knows What Else – my own diagnosis. He had black tousled hair, dark eyes with long lashes and a big gold earring in each ear. His dark eyes had a faraway appearance and he had a wild look about him. Scruffy, always in the same smelly, stained, old yellow jumper. His language would have made the roughest diamond flinch. Jordan was also achingly vulnerable.

Today was a really bad day for the young lad. He had probably been up half the night watching totally inappropriate TV programmes or playing on overstimulating computer games all night with his older brothers. His mum was probably out turning tricks so she could pay her bills or pulling pints at The Black Dog and lining up her next waste-of-space new bloke.

We did our best with Jordan and other kids like him at school. But we knew our limitations. We knew that whatever calm and stability we gave him during the school day, would be totally overturned when the bell rang at the end of the afternoon.

Jordan would not be met off the school bus by a

responsible adult or loving, supportive parent. He would hop off the bus, amble around the streets for a bit or hang around the dodgy local park. He would then head home to a chaotic household where he was fed coke, crisps, sweets, biscuits and other junk food, guaranteed to send his blood sugar, behaviour and stress levels through the roof.

Jordan spent most of the school holidays, evenings and weekends riding around aimlessly on an old racing bike. His grandad had cobbled it together for him from odd bits of old bikes found in skips and against dustbins. Despite his limited intelligence and special educational needs, Jordan somehow negotiated the busy roads where he lived and managed to stay alive.

If I sat and thought too hard about the lack of quality and care in Jordan's life, I could have wept each day. Jordan was the "Timothy Winters" of our day. No love, no money, no care. You did what you could, but goodness knows how a kid like that was ever going to have much of a life. No hope, no motivation, no change for the better. Just survival for Jordan and his family.

I watched as he tormented another child and was remonstrated by Marion, my lovely teaching assistant. Marion was told promptly to "fuck off" by an increasingly angry and frustrated Jordan.

We were singing the song "Love Is All Around" by Wet, Wet, Wet, in honour of Valentine's Day. We were nothing but ambitious! *Not much love around for Jordan with his unkempt tousled curls, probably nurturing lice at this very moment, and stained, too-tight jumper*, I thought sadly. *Not much love for me either*, I reflected. No card, no flowers, not even a romantic, loving message. No call, no promise of a call. No "I love you, Delphy, wish I could be with you today, darling". Nothing.

I tried to concentrate on the children and push away the thought that Jenny would have been given a nice card and probably some flowers from Ben. I tried to ignore the idea that Ben might take his wife out for a nice meal that evening, even though they rarely did go out together socially. It wasn't that I had been ignored. I had received the usual messages from Ben throughout the day. "Good morning, off to work. Have a good day" and "Yes, I'm OK. Off to a meeting, busy day. Hope you are well. How's it going?".

All perfectly nice messages, yet I was upset all the same. I was hurt that Ben didn't think to wish me a Happy Valentine's Day and send me a *special* message. I felt ignored, neglected, forgotten. I knew he was busy, but he was always busy. I felt childish, needy and a little pathetic that it meant so much to me, but we had been together for well over a year at that point.

We had a proper, *intimate* relationship and were an established couple, in so far as we could be. I felt I was his loved one, the *special* one, and I wanted to hear it on the very day that red hearts and roses were all around us. Surely, he would notice the flowers everywhere, advertisements for chocolates and cards, restaurants and shops dressed up for St. Valentine's and think of me? Romantic songs were all over the radio. Love really was all around us that day. Surely, he would think of me and us? Of course, I said none of this. A romantic gesture is not the same if asked for or intimated. I did not want to put any more pressure on an already stressed Ben. I could not appear needy, high maintenance nor demanding. Those were against the rules.

So, I put on my smiley mask and messaged back as if it was any other day. "Good morning, you, yes I'm fine, but having a very difficult day in classroom. But that's special needs teaching for you. Hope your day goes well".

Jordan's behaviour was escalating as he became more and more out of control. Marion had coped well with him as usual but had now had more than enough. She told him to take time out and stand outside the classroom for five minutes. Jordan needed to cool down and we all needed a break from him for a few moments. He was so wearing when he was like this.

I decided to give Marion a break and, after a quick chat to explain what the rest of the class was doing, went into the corridor to check on Jordan and try to reason with him a little. Easier said than done. There was a strong possibility that he may not have been given his medication. I thought I'd better ask the school secretary to phone home to check on this. There was a chance that his mum may just about have tumbled out of bed. She may even have remembered whether her son had been given his calming pills.

Jordan was not there. Not again. I did a quick check in the loos and around the corridors. Nowhere to be seen. I went back into the classroom and spoke with Marion. She looked horrified and as if she was about to break down in floods of tears. Marion had problems of her own. Struggling with the menopause, hot flushes and flooding (I wonder if Penny is writing poems about those now...?), her husband had been out of work for six months and her daughter was playing up at school. Poor Marion – life can be very hard. I was often glad to be single, relatively carefree and uncomplicated. Well, that was pre-Ben anyway.

I tried to calm Marion.

'It's not your fault, Marion, please don't feel bad. He's a handful. Look, you go to the caretaker – ask him to scout around all the buildings. If he's not on school premises, we'll report to the head and then call mum. Jordan walked all the way back home once. It's only a short bus ride for him, and he knows the local streets like the back of his hands. He rides around them enough on that racing bike of his.'

Usual routine, search party Jordan. Not that his family gave a damn. His mum was probably more annoyed that she had to roll out of bed and say goodbye to her latest squeeze. Or leave the pub early. Or miss her favourite reality afternoon TV or quiz show. It took over two hours to locate Jordan. He said he had been hiding in one of the school cupboards for a while and then went walkabout. He was eventually found asleep in a bus shelter just across the road.

Marion and I were hauled into the head's office and given a real ticking off. Apparently, we were negligent and careless. How did he get out? Why did it take so long to track him down? Marion was crying again by the end of it, poor cow. She had enough on her plate, was paid a pittance and could do without this.

I was angry, more than anything, at the lack of support we had been shown. There was no acknowledgement of the stress and worry we had experienced. No support of Marion and I, professionals doing a difficult job. I sat there quietly while the head went on and on. I took it all on the chin for both of us. I would have to fill in hours of forms and reports over this incident. I would stay up all night and do them as soon as I eventually got home.

I would do them at once just so that I had the satisfaction of banging them on the head's desk first thing tomorrow morning. How dare she question my care of the children and my professionalism?

I decided to request a meeting the next day with the head and Jordan's mother, Sandra. It needed to be aired how difficult Jordan was becoming, largely because he was not given his medication regularly at home. I planned to explain how the disintegration of his behaviour was detrimental, not just to himself but to others in the class. Not to mention the teaching staff. Jordan had always pushed limits, but he was becoming unmanageable, and this had to be addressed for all our sakes.

I disliked the new headteacher. She was out to make a name for herself, and this job was a mere stepping stone to a career within the LEA as an Educational Consultant. She didn't care about the school, the children, nor the staff. She was not smart nor committed; she was manipulative and played the game. A long player who had clawed her way up the teaching ladder, by saying and doing all the right things to the right people at the top.

She did not present as a primary headteacher. Short skirts, high heels, flashy jewellery, fake smile. One of the other staff members joked that she must set her alarm for five each morning in time to apply so much make-up. And probably without a mirror. *Miaow!* She had a scary china doll face with bright red, blobby-blushed cheeks, garish stripes of dark blue eyeshadow and long, black false lashes. Her eyebrows looked like two thick caterpillars had died on her forehead. She looked ridiculous but obviously thought she looked glamorous and amazing. *Miaow!*

Bitching aside, and more importantly, she showed absolutely no support or empathy towards her staff. She had a total lack of awareness when dealing with a kid like Jordan. Too young and inexperienced to be a head, no significant background in special education. She probably only agreed to have a special unit on the school premises to gain a few brownie points with the LEA and had no idea of the responsibilities she and the school were taking on in doing so. *Miaow again!*

It was a rough day. I was extremely relieved that Jordan was OK. I decided to pop by his house on my way home, just to check on him and to have a supportive chat with mum, Sandra, ahead of a more formal meeting. I did not agree with the way she lived her life or dragged up her kids. I also understood that life was not exactly straightforward for her. I had come to know her quite well over the last year that I had been teaching her son. She appreciated that I was sympathetic, would hear her out and that I liked and tried to do all I could for her boy. More importantly, she knew that I did not talk down to her but spoke to her straightforwardly and on equal terms.

Sandra was probably on the autistic spectrum herself and had all sorts of mental health issues that had never been diagnosed nor treated. A friendly chat would go a long way towards making her feel less alienated and defensive, and probably prevent her from making a formal complaint against the school. She would want to detract from her own inadequate parenting and subsequent guilt so may start hitting out. Damage and stress limitation. Something the new head would never have even considered, despite her huge salary, nodding, smiling china doll face, and flashy gold and diamond rings on every finger. *Double miaow!*

Sandra seemed pleased to see me and our chat went well. When I finally made it home, I had a simple omelette for supper and a comforting mug of hot chocolate. I checked my phone before I settled down to writing a report on the day's events. I would be working until midnight at the very least and had another full day ahead. But at least it was Friday tomorrow. I had a weekend of lie-ins to look forward to. Bliss.

So, it was official, no Happy Valentine's message for me today. Nothing. Just a "Back home now, looking forward to a nice supper and feet up for a few hours. Work is mental busy. You OK?".

I ignored the message. Was he really that ignorant? How could he possibly have got through today without noticing it was Valentine's Day? It was on the TV, the radio, newspapers, bloody everywhere. Did he not open a card from his wife that morning? I got on with my report and worked well into the night. Finished at twelve-thirty. Checked phone again. He had not said goodnight. Probably because he could see that I had read, but not responded to, his boring message.

It was all a game really, I sometimes thought. That kind of extra, long-distance, part-real, part-fantasy relationship. Ben often went to bed very late, so perhaps he was not ignoring me in return. I dithered over the phone and wondered whether I ought to ignore his perceived neglect of me and say goodnight in a grown-up fashion. Or perhaps ask him outright, or at least in a funny, flirty way, why he had not sent me anything romantic on a day set aside for lovers?

It seemed a bit pathetic to ask and I did not want to seem needy nor upset him, so I just typed "Goodnight". But then because I was hurt, felt resentful and, yes, I can be extremely childish when offended or slighted, I typed "Oh... and Happy Fucking Valentine's Day. Thanks for not bothering as usual". No kisses obviously. I pressed send and switched off my phone. Fuck him, I didn't care about his response.

It had been a dreadful day and, as ever, you were not there for me.

I was not able to call him when I needed to, could not talk to him about what had happened at work that day. Ben had probably had a nice, relaxing evening watching TV with Jenny, maybe a romcom. There would be two Valentine's cards on the mantelpiece and, most likely, a bouquet of red roses in a vase on the coffee table. I knew this because I had visited him at their home last February, when Jenny was away visiting her mother.

I had tried not to look at the vase of red roses alongside the two cards. One of the cards had a photograph of a rabbit with a big red bow on the front. I guessed it was Jenny's card for Ben. He had a thing about rabbits, for some reason. Thought they were dead cute. I remember thinking that it was the sort of "obvious" card I hated, more like a birthday card for a nan or elderly aunt.

I would never have given that card to Ben.

I looked around their home that day. I saw the way Jenny was dressed in the few photos on display and could not help noticing how frumpy she was. She had certainly let herself go and looked older than her years. Funny, I had always considered Ben to be a stylish guy. He always wore good clothes when we were younger, still had impeccable taste in music and films, and read intelligent, cultured books. I kept my opinions to myself, of course, and felt slightly bad about judging the tastes of a woman whose husband I regularly stole away from her. I also pretended not to notice the little expressions of love and coupledom around the room. Little signs telling each other that they were *best friends forever*, mugs with *my lovely husband* and *my one and only* emblazoned across them. I placed a big smile on my face to hide my disappointment and hurt. My mask.

Jenny was probably snuggled up with him right now, I thought, stuffing her face with the extra chocolates he had bought her this year. *Guilty gifts to compensate for sleeping with another woman*, I thought harshly. The bitter, negative thoughts persisted despite my *I don't care, I'm strong and independent* mask.

I checked the clock. It was very late, so they would be in bed now, asleep together. Would they have made love, despite Ben telling me they never did? I blanked that thought. But the image of them snuggled together over flowers, cards, and now even chocolates stayed with me as I clambered, totally exhausted, into my own bed.

A message, a card, a little *I love you*, a thought. Such tiny details should not be that important in the grand scheme of things, but they are. They constitute the fabric of a relationship and are particularly important when you are clinging onto threads.

Shame on you, Ben, I thought. *Shame on you. I thought you would value me more. Why do you never come up trumps these days? Just for once.*

Dillon comes onto Suzie

There was trouble in the band. Ben and Suzie's relationship had always been rocky, but the last few months it had hit boiling point. If either of them had any sense, they would have stopped seeing each other months ago. But I had noticed that Ben was not very good at ending relationships. He could not seem to let go; consequently, his relationships dragged out way beyond the point of pleasure. When things were slipping away, it was best to call it quits and say goodbye before the hurt went too deep. Otherwise, both parties ended up blaming and deeply resenting each other, and there was no chance of future friendship.

Ben had been in a funny mood during the last few band rehearsals. He always went quiet on us when he was upset about anything. I asked if he was OK, but he shrugged and said nothing. Always so annoying when you feel you are close to someone and can see something is wrong, but they won't let you in. But that was Ben. He could be difficult like that.

Personally, I was growing tired of Ben's moods and the whole Ben/Suzie drama, so I did not press him further. We all did our best to ignore his sulky moods and concentrated on rehearsals. We had a gig to practise and plan for and did not need distractions. We usually went for a drink together at the end of a rehearsal. The band would sit around and chat about how the evening had panned out and talk through new material or an upcoming gig.

Suzie usually joined us at some point, but she had not made an appearance that evening.

To be perfectly frank, I felt quite pleased when Suzie was not there. I found her childish, tiresome and boring. I did not feel she brought out the best in Ben – he was different when she was around and less fun.

We sat together in our favourite corner of The Old Snug Tavern when Dillon walked in. *Oh God, that's all we need*, I thought. He was on his own – his short-lived relationship with Suzie's cousin, Becky, had fizzled out soon after the picnic. Dillon spotted us immediately, came straight over and asked if he could join us.

'Yeah sure,' I said, hoping he would not stay too long.

'So, you and Suzie finished now then?' Dillon asked Ben.

'What the fuck has it got to do with you?' replied Ben tersely.

God, he was stressed and easily riled at times.

'Alright mate, I was just asking. I saw her earlier and she looked a bit upset, that's all.'

'Where did you see her?' Ben demanded.

'Walking along by the park and looking a bit lonely. She told me you had finished.'

It was obviously news to Ben.

'Yeah, I offered her a lift home. Didn't expect her to be quite so grateful,' he smirked, looking directly at Ben.

Ben flushed up. 'You what…?'

'Yeah, the quiet girls are always the insatiable ones.'

Ben jumped up. 'You fucking lying…'

Dillon just stood there and started laughing at him.

'Alright, calm down a bit, mate! I'm only messing with you. Not really my type anyway, your Suzie. You're welcome to her. Prefer them a bit slimmer and leggier. And less desperate.'

'Why don't you piss off, Dillon.' That was me.

I could see Ben was tightly coiled and I never did like seeing him upset, even back then when we were younger.

I was also feeling some tensions in the band, and I wanted to knock it on the head before it became too deeply set in. Bands, famous or otherwise, often broke up because of silly, petty squabbles that got out of hand. I loved The Thistles and I felt we were really coming together and into our own. We had some great new songs, were playing live fairly regularly and even earnt a bit of cash sometimes.

And I loved *being in a band*. I loved the camaraderie with the guys. I loved our music, finding venues, putting together playlists, promoting, choosing stage outfits, even travelling in the van. I was studying hard, and doing as many extra shifts as I could fit in at Woollies to save for a car and go away to study for my degree. I *needed* The Thistles. It gave me an outlet and a bit of fun. I would really miss the band if we finished, particularly if it was over something ridiculous and not even that important.

Unfortunately, most of our rows were over something ridiculous and not even that important.

It used to get me down a lot.

'Yeah, piss off,' Ben chipped in. Dillon laughed, downed his pint theatrically, then walked over to the other bar to annoy someone else.

'I'm sure he fancies her,' said Ben. 'He's been hanging around Suzie ever since Becky dropped him.'

'Take no notice, Ben. Dillon always wants what he can't have. He only misses the band because I'm singing with you now and he can't come back. If she's worth anything, she won't be in the least bit interested in him. She's got you, hasn't she? Dillon's vacuous.'

Ben smiled at me. We had different opinions about many things and bickered quite a bit about band stuff and the world in general. But Ben understood that I was basically on his side and would always have his corner. I smiled back at him. I did feel like the mother hen of the group at times, forever advising on relationships and giving them all tips on how to treat girls. It was simple really, I said, just be nice to us and don't play games. They all looked completely out of their depth – if only they realised we were just as unsure and wary of them.

No one likes being vulnerable. Putting yourself in the hands of someone else and hoping and trusting they will look after your heart is a risky business. It was a wonder anyone ever got together at all really. I remember looking at married couples and thinking that it was all going to get a lot easier when I was a mature, grown-up woman. Then suddenly I'm heading towards forty and still feel as confused and vulnerable as that little sixth former. Excited, optimistic, yet terrified of the prospect of stepping out into the big wide world outside of Cowlington.

Two weeks later, we had a gig organised at The Blackbird, a pub with a lovely, large back room with great acoustics. We had a comedian as support, Bernie Goldburn. He was pretty good, got a lot of laughs and warmed the audience up nicely for us. Suzie was standing at the back with her cousin Becky and a few friends. Penny was there too, with her new (not married and not sleazy) boyfriend. There were quite a few there, including Keithie and a few other musicians from local bands we sometimes played with. Graham from Little Black Kitten, Billy from Pigeon Feet.

And then I spotted him. Dillon. He walked in, looked at Ben and went straight over to Suzie. Ben looked up, quickly looked away again and focused on getting ready to play. We were just about to start the gig. I went over to Ben.

'You OK?'

He nodded.

'You and Suzie made up?'

'I thought so, yes.'

'It's not her fault he turned up. Just ignore them both and concentrate on giving a great performance, OK?'

'I'll try.'

'No, you'll do it. It's not just about you, Ben – you're part of this band and you can't let us down.'

'Yes, Mama Delphy. Point noted.' He crinkled a smile despite himself.

Even then I remember thinking what a cheeky, attractive smile he had. I glanced over at Ian, who raised his eyebrows but visibly relaxed when I gave him a quick thumbs up.

We were as ready as we could be. We had been rehearsing rigorously for weeks. I had been off for half-term so had more time to practise. As usual we had a punk sound, but we threw in a folksy number and a slow, haunting song just to mix it up a bit. We were going to end with "Firechaser", a hectic, crazy number co-written by Ian and Ben. It was guaranteed to get the audience pogoing and would end the evening on a wild, high note.

The guys wore black trousers or jeans with white T-shirts emblazoned with their favourite band names. I wore a red mini shift dress with sheer black dotty tights (you could get some great tights in the eighties) and black monkey boots. Kind of new wave/tomboy glam. Dark, smoky eye make-up (trying my best to look as mysterious as Siouxsie) and customary messy bob (trying my best to look as cool as Debbie Harry). I'd just had my hair cut a little shorter, so this was a new, experimental look for me, and I was pretty pleased with it.

Richie's dad took some photos whilst we were playing, and we looked pretty cool together. We were finally beginning to establish a stronger visual image and our own identity. Unfortunately, having our own unique sound was a different matter, and I never felt we achieved that.

I could see Dillon leaning into Suzie and whispering in her ear. She smiled and nodded, and he went off to the bar and came back with a drink for her. She did not seem to be discouraging him in the least, throwing her head back and giggling at everything he said.

I could never remember him being quite that funny. I hoped it was worth putting up with him for a free cider and black.

I was not keen on Dillon. He came from a fairly affluent background by Cowlington standards. Nothing wrong with having a bit of money, but Dillon was flash with his cash and very full of himself for no reason at all, which was not fine. He seemed to think he could buy his way into anywhere and do anything he wanted. Well, not The Thistles. He wasn't buying back into us, whatever deal he came up with. He had too much ego and caused divisions that could easily be the death of any group.

I glanced over at Ben and was pleased to see him focused on playing. He was not even noticeably looking towards the back of the hall where Dillon and Suzie were huddling. Even as a young man, Ben could be detached when he felt it was necessary. A coping mechanism learnt early on, I guessed. Perfected later in life.

We played enthusiastically, if not well, to a warm,

boisterous and encouraging crowd. It was a Wednesday evening, in the middle of the working week, so nobody was particularly drunk, just lively. Apart from Keithie, of course, who never worked and was obviously on something. But Keithie was chilled rather than rowdy. He stood apart from the crowd, swaying languidly, with a big curled-up smile on his face. I waved and blew him a kiss and he waved back.

Towards the end of the set, I took in the hall. Dillon now had his arm around Suzie and was looking directly at Ben. Suzie seemed to be loving the attention, the chance to wind up Ben and fuel his jealousy. She was immature, as I thought, and enjoying playing games with Ben's feelings. I found her irritating and wished they would both leave as their presence was spoiling a great evening.

We finished the set and played "Never sleep with an ex" as an encore. Rather appropriate, I remember thinking. It was a song I wrote after watching a TV play. I have never thought it was a good idea to revisit a romantic relationship once it's over. Once it's over, it's over. Finish, walk away, don't try to stay friends unless you really must and certainly don't get drunk together or sleep together again. If it's bad sex you will regret it; if it's great sex you will have a sad reminder of what you have lost. And regret it. It becomes a bad habit. Better to move on – there's a whole world of new potential partners and future exes out there.

As soon as we finished, Ben leapt off the stage towards the direction of Suzie and Dillon.

Ian looked concerned but stayed put. I started to move towards the front of the stage, but Ian put his hand on my arm.

'Just leave them,' he said. 'It's nothing to do with us, Delphy. Let them sort it out themselves. I know you worry about him, but Ben's a grown-up.'

That was debatable, I thought, particularly where Suzie and Dillon were concerned.

A few minutes later, Ben had pushed Dillon against the wall. Dillon could have floored Ben with one punch, and we all knew that. Instead, he raised his arms, as if it was not worth the effort and just laughed at him. Poor Ben – Dillon was humiliating him.

Suzie started shouting and pulling Ben away, then Ben started shouting at them both. Becky got involved and started shouting at Ben. Dillon just stood there grinning, enjoying his evening's work and all the upset he was causing, like a demented, contemporary Iago. *Othello* was one of my set texts, so I knew how this all worked…

Ben suddenly grabbed Suzie's hand and they left together, leaving us to pack up all his stuff. He turned up about an hour later, having walked Suzie home. We were packing up the van and about to head off.

'Nice of you to show up, mate. We packed up your gear for you.' That was Richie. He was not impressed, having little patience with drama and histrionics.

Ben said he was sorry, but he had to sort things out with Suzie and get her back home safely. He was good like that, kind of old-fashioned and chivalrous, despite the way she treated him. She was upset; he obviously still cared for her and continued to feel protective towards her.

'I hope she's worth it, Ben,' I said quietly. 'Because she certainly seems like a lot of trouble to me.'

Ben smiled wanly and said nothing. I said no more. I didn't mention Dillon had been snogging Suzie's cousin, Becky, five minutes after they had left.

Chasing dreams

Flying, flying high
Don't want to come down
I sense the magic has gone
But just can't come down now

I'm still flying high
Don't want to come down
Down to where it's real
I just can't give you up

Chasing dreams
Though I need to sleep
Laughing, smiling, singing
When I should fall down and weep

It's so much fun up here
Like it was at the very start
Can't just can't stop now
Because I'd have to admit

That we're falling apart
Yes, we're falling apart...

We had a row, of course, after the Valentine's Day message, or lack of. You thought I was being ridiculous, overly dramatic, overly sensitive. You were busy, out early, didn't even really think of it. Yes, you had left Jenny a card, no flowers this year though, you said.

You did not say sorry because you did not think it was important and did not understand why I was upset. I silently fumed and ignored you for a bit longer. I'm turning into Suzie, I thought, worryingly. Yet still it hurt.

By the afternoon of the next day, you suggested we talk on the phone when you had finished work and asked if I was free. I agreed we should talk it through. I always looked forward to speaking with you and was glad to hear your voice.

But I could not help thinking that if only we were able to talk properly, more regularly and freely, we would not constantly have these misunderstandings. We would be more in tune and easy with each other, as we always used to be.

I had assumed that we had a natural connection that most people did not have, but I was beginning to question this now. Maybe my imagination and memory had distorted our relationship and it could never live up to the inflated importance I had wrongly given it?

I often thought that having a phone conversation with Ben was more akin to undertaking a military operation. OK, we both worked, and I did not want to interrupt his working day, nor he mine. However, he was either at work or home with Jenny and Rachael. He did not have any hobbies, social activities, or seem able to go out of the house on his own unless he was working. This made it impossible to call him for a casual chat in the spontaneous way I did with other friends.

As a single, grown-up woman, I was finding this increasingly restrictive and frustrating.

The prison he had built for himself was becoming my prison.

We often did not see each other for several weeks. I missed him so much, but Ben never seemed to manage even a weekly phone call. If I hadn't seen Mum and Dad, Sandy or Neil for a week or so, we always rang each other and had a proper chat. We loved and missed one another and liked to hear each other's voices. I spoke to most of my girlfriends more than I spoke with Ben.

He seemed content with daily messaging which I hated. I found it impersonal, distant and prone to misunderstandings and miscommunication. I also found a lot of Ben's messages mundane and dull.

Ben seemed like another person in text form. The man I thought I knew so intimately became a stranger to me, reduced to words, punctuation and the odd joke, if he was feeling frivolous. I longed for a flirty, sexy, romantic message – something that extended our emotional and physical attachment. Ben argued that messaging *feelings* made him feel uncomfortable and diluted his emotional attachment to me. That sounded very noble, but I also thought, *What a load of old bollocks!*

It seemed more like an excuse for someone who wanted to stay detached and to express emotions on his terms only. I saw it as an unwillingness to do something that I thought was necessary to nurture our relationship. It was something that I needed to stay connected and happy with him. And yet it was ignored.

Intervals between calls were so drawn out that I went beyond looking forward to them. Instead, I felt disappointed with him for not finding time for me or angry that I had been kept waiting so long. When a call was finally arranged, it was always at a time most convenient for Ben. I found myself rushing through admin after work, watching the clock at meetings, getting a later train, just so that I could be available on the rare occasion that Ben was free to talk to me.

Sometimes I had been missing him so much that it physically hurt. He always seemed unaffected. 'I miss you too,' he assured me, but was able to "compartmentalise his feelings", whatever that meant. I wish I could have done that too.

Occasionally, a feeling of resentment would build up inside me and his calls would feel like "duty calls". Something he felt he was expected to do to keep the relationship going, but did not personally need, enjoy nor have the time for. Ben often sounded flat, fed up and talked a lot about work and family problems on the phone.

I was beginning to feel he had the ability to rinse the joy out of everything, even what should have been a precious call between long-distance lovers. I would try to flirt with him, just as when we were younger, have a bit of fun and turn the focus onto us. But Ben always referred back to work, the business and his never-ending stresses, difficulties and many problems. There wasn't a lot of fun with Ben anymore!

He was obviously not happy with his life, but, looking back, he almost seemed to enjoy a bit of wallowing in misery, even as a young man. He did love to moan! Not me. I was afraid of sinking down. I had seen what depression could do, as there was a lot of it on my mother's side. I liked to keep things buoyant, keep life as joyful and light-hearted as possible. It was important in my work too, to keep the darkness at bay.

Dealing with the kids I worked with on a daily basis, with all their personal and family problems, social neglect and sometimes sheer pain and misery, it was very important to stay on the right side of positive.

In truth, and although I was reluctant to admit it even to myself, I was beginning to feel dragged down by Ben's perpetual doom and gloom. Fairly early on in our relationship, I began to wonder if he was really making me happy. But then something good would happen between us. We would have a nice day; he would be romantic and loving towards me once again. And it would all seem worthwhile.

But that's how junkies exist, don't they? They live for the fix, the rush, the high. For me, it was the drip, drip, drip of love and affection that kept me going. I would ache for Ben for weeks and just when I could not bear it much longer, he would tell me how much he loved me, or we would meet up and talk and laugh and kiss... and it would all feel wonderful again.

I had my fix and that kept me hooked in for the next dry spell.

If I had been honest with myself at that time, I would have accepted that Ben was not making me happy. I was just like Jordan's mum, hooked in by promises and false dreams from a man who was not emotionally available but just could not let me go. And I could not let him go. Maybe that's why I could sympathise with Sandra when others could not. I understood that once you've fallen in love madly and deeply, you desperately cling onto the dream of what was and what could have been – if only the circumstances and timing had been different.

And, if the object of your passion seems to grow a little detached, a little cool, pulls away and seems less interested, you can become addicted to trying to return to that glowing idyll of newness and excitement. The oxytocin-fuelled sheer pleasure of those early stolen kisses and increasing desire that raises an average, not particularly special, middling man way above his worth. The relationship, although unsatisfying and growing increasingly toxic, continues way beyond its sell-by date.

We had a long chat on the phone.

Of course, you talked me round. You told me how important I was to you… you had waited such a long time for me. You loved me, had always loved me. It was all I ever wanted to hear. I smiled through my tears. I hated rowing with you. It made me feel physically sick and affected my sleep. When we had fallen out, I would wake with a deep gnaw in my stomach and a leaden heart. You said that you also felt unhappy when things were not right with us. So, I wondered, why could you not act a little more loving towards me and return my attention and affection more equally? Why could you not give me a little bit more, so that we still had that special something that reeled me in at the start?

As I put down the phone, I tried to ignore that little heart flutter that demanded why Ben had not called me before. Why did we even get to the stage where I was upset or quiet before he was reminded that we had not spoken for weeks? Yes, weeks. Why would he not want to talk to me? Did he not miss me the way I missed him? Why was it so much easier for him? 'I'm closed. I don't like to dilute my feelings for you. I don't disclose my emotions that easily. The significance of feelings is lost if they are talked about too much. It's not necessary to share emotions; I keep them to myself.'

I understood that you were closed and naturally far less open than me. But you were certainly more open in the beginning. It was you who suggested we met, just the two of us, you who told me you loved and had always been in love with me. It was you who offered that first kiss. I understood that maybe you needed to compartmentalise to have an affair and that you were trying to juggle things so that everyone was kept happy. I knew that you did not have much of a marriage. I knew you were desperate to do the "right" thing by your family whilst having me in your life. I accepted that compromise and would never demand that you give up Jenny and Rachael for me. I knew the guilt and shame would destroy you and probably ruin our relationship too.

But what about my feelings? Why did he suddenly change after those first few heady months? It couldn't all be about work. He said it wasn't guilt. He said he could be quite cold about that kind of thing, was able to box his feelings and justify matters for his own needs. He had not been happy with Jenny for years before he met me again. He did not feel she was his soulmate or "special one". That was me apparently. The missing piece. The last part of the jigsaw. His home. He told me of my significance to him at the very start.

But where were we now? We had been together for more than a year, and he seemed wary, pushing me away, reluctant to express his feelings for me. I didn't understand what had changed and I felt as if I was going mad at times. I knew something was different; I could feel it.

Or maybe I was feeling the chill of your coldness as you distanced yourself so that you would never be tempted to overly commit to me or get too close. I didn't know, I really didn't. But I was so tired of trying to understand you and so tired of feeling disappointed by you. I sometimes wondered whether you were not as smart and emotionally intelligent as I thought you were... or perhaps this was a straightforward case of Venus and Mars? The gender divide – but there I was again, making excuses for you instead of facing up to the truth.

You didn't seem to understand what I needed. Or maybe you had changed more than I thought and were no longer the Ben I remembered? I worried again whether or not I could tell you everything. I did not think I could tell you what had happened. I was no longer sure you loved me enough to be trusted with that information.

Time had passed and you seemed hardened, embittered, able to easily process and box your feelings. You seemed cold and brittle-hearted. The sort of man who could have affairs without too much personal torment, despite what you sometimes told me. I wondered if I really knew you at all, but still, to my shame and disbelief, I could not quite let you go. I really could not.

Swimming pool

When we had finished Thursday night band practice, we always went for a drink. Occasionally it was just the three of us, Ian, Ben and me. We always got on well and had a good laugh. Weirdly, I generally chatted (or argued!) with Ben more than I did with my boyfriend, Ian, who was the quietest of the three of us. There was never any tension over it; in fact, I think Ian was quite happy that Ben and I got on so well. It meant his best mate didn't feel left out and he could spend time with us both.

We were usually quite drunk by the time we were walking back home. We all had to rush to get to band practice after work, so there was not much time for food. I did an extra evening shift at Woollies on Thursdays after school, so tea was usually a bar of chocolate, as I legged it to the practice hall. Then a bag of crisps in the pub later. And a few beers.

On the way home towards the chip shop, we always passed the big, posh houses by the park. We weren't quite "born in a shoebox on't road", but none of us came from much, so we could hardly believe that some people not only had five or six bedrooms (we all had to share as kids) but also patios, conservatories, drives and their own parking. Luxury. The corner house particularly fascinated us because it had a swimming pool. The only private house we had ever seen with one.

After one spectacularly bad rehearsal, we had a few bevies too many and were livelier than usual. We generally had a bit of a sing-song on the way home from the pub. This time we walked quietly, moaning about the others for being so boring and never wanting to ring the changes or do anything new. The three of us were still concerned that The Thistles did not have a strong sound of its own, but the others did not have a strong sound of its own, but the others did not seem overly bothered in addressing what we felt was holding us back. We thought certain local bands, with their own clearly defined sound, were making better progress than we were. Pigeon Feet recently clinched an interview and a few songs on the local radio which had made us more than a little envious.

And, as usual, Ben was unhappy about his relationship with Suzie. I never knew what they found to argue about, but maybe later I came to realise why she never seemed happy with him. Perhaps even at that young age, he could not give enough of himself? Perhaps Ben could not commit to anyone?

'I hate the people in that house,' pronounced Ben, fed up with himself, the band, his girlfriend and looking for a vent. 'I hate their garden, their posh cars and their poxy swimming pool.'

'You don't even know them, Ben!' I laughed at him. He could be randomly vitriolic at times.

'I know, but it just annoys me that a lot of people around here don't even have a job, don't have a pot to piss in and they're flaunting all this ridiculous wealth... I'm sick of it.'

It was the early eighties, Thatcher's Britain. A few years later, the economy would really pick up. Everyone would start wearing ridiculous shoulder pads, have huge hair, big chunky gold earrings and clasp enormous mobile phones to their ears. *Loadsamoney.*

But when we were in our teens, it was hard for most people to get a decent job after leaving school. More and more local firms were closing and loads of dads lost their jobs – men were generally the main breadwinners where we lived.

Ben had a point, of course, but he always took everything very personally and to extremes.

I saw him glance at Ian with his mischievous grin and then they suddenly both legged it over the fence. I was left standing anxiously on my own, wondering what on earth they were up to now.

'What the hell…?' I looked around nervously.

I may have sung in a punk band and had a bit of attitude – my latest school report had said I was becoming truculent. I had to look this up and I must say I did not feel insulted. There is quite a lot to be truculent about when you are eighteen. However, I was generally a good girl and did not like to get into trouble.

I couldn't believe it when I saw them throwing one of the posh couple's patio chairs into their pool. A light went on; a dog barked; someone shouted out.

'Quick, someone's coming!' I hissed.

Ben looked around and quickly threw another chair in for good measure. I was up the road already and rolled my eyes as I heard the splash. They both jumped over the fence, absolutely killing themselves with laughter, as we ran off to the chippy for a bag of chips each. With extra salt and vinegar of course – no one seemed to worry about arteries in those days. Well, not in Cowlington, anyway.

I'm afraid to say that was not the first incident concerning the posh house on the corner. It became a regular thing when Ben and Ian got drunk – to chuck a chair in their pool. They were never caught, mainly because I was a much better looker-outer than Ian, but it finally came to a head when the whole band walked home together one Thursday night and all the guys jumped over. Sorry to say, all six chairs and the actual table went into the pool after one particularly raucous evening in the pub. Poor Ian was laughing so much that he very nearly did not make it back over onto the safety of the pavement.

It was so funny that I was nearly sick, but I did feel guilty every time I walked past and saw the perfectly decent-looking, middle-aged couple sitting on their patio by their pool. It wasn't their fault that they had a lot of money when many others did not even have a job. The guys never did it again. The joke hit a crescendo once the whole suite went in. But I did notice all the furniture was chained down the next time I walked by. That made me smile. Kids can be a bloody nuisance at times. But hey, rock and roll.

Eggshells

You wonder why I'm quiet
You wonder why I'm sad
Why it feels like you
Are treading eggshells
Why I'm always getting mad

Well, you text "Hello" in the morning
And you text me back "Goodnight"
And we hardly ever talk
And none of this feels right.

I no longer feel very special
We slipped into routine so soon
You settle for the ordinary
I yearn for the stars and the moon.

I always looked forward to my birthday. Last year we had not long been together, but you made a fuss of me anyway. You suggested we meet up to celebrate on the day, but I was working and couldn't, and you weren't able to get away for the evening. But you called me and left a really nice voicemail, and you sang "Happy birthday" to me down the phone. It was so lovely to hear your voice even if I could not be with you on my special day. I played it back several times during the day and I loved it. We met up the following week and you took me for lunch and gave me a thoughtful selection of CDs as a gift. They were well chosen and personal. It was a lovely present. We had a wonderful day together, as we always did that first year.

The time we spent together was so important to me. It meant that I could put up with the fact you were not wholly mine and we would probably never spend the rest of our lives together. We would have both loved this, I was sure, if things had been different. I think if you had asked me to throw in everything, my job, my flat and just sail away with you, I would have gone, despite my logical, sensible, feminist side screaming at me to think this through. I was quite besotted with you.

I still had not talked to you about what happened. Each time I came close, something intervened to change my mind. I had not talked about it to anyone in such a long time; I was not sure I wanted to open it all up again. Yet I felt so close to you, it seemed like a betrayal not to share significant experiences with you. The good, the bad, the ugly. The stuff that made me who I had become. I wanted to share it all with you and keep nothing from you.

Towards the end of our second year together, my birthday fell on the weekend, so of course I would not be seeing Ben. But he hadn't mentioned anything anyway. I was conscious that we did not have any dates in the diary to meet up that month, and I had barely seen him during the summer. There was always something. As a teacher, I had a nice, long summer break and the previous year Ben had taken quite a few days off to be with me. It had been a fabulous summer and we somehow managed to spend lots of time together. I loved it.

I felt then that our relationship had significantly grown and deepened during those summer months, and we had, at last, got into some kind of routine of seeing each other regularly. We did not have to rely on interminable messaging to keep in contact.

"Morning, how are you? Have a good day".

"Are you OK? Sorry, mental busy at moment".

"Sorry, no time to talk".

"Sorry, in a meeting".

"Sorry, sitting with Jen and Rachael. Give me some dates, I'll do my best".

"Can't really talk, difficult. Can I have those dates again? I deleted by mistake".

"Sorry, frantic day. Can't talk, Jenny at home".

"Can you let me have those dates again, sorry, deleted all your messages to be on safe side".

"Off to bed, night, sorry not been in touch much".

This summer it had been messages, messages, messages punctuated by the odd meet-up. We rarely talked properly. Work was obviously problematic and very full-on, but he never seemed to have time for me anymore. If I ever said anything to him about the long and unsatisfactory absences, he became very defensive and we either had a row, or he stonewalled me. But it was becoming increasingly difficult for me to manage the time apart from Ben. I missed him terribly. When he was busy (always), not only did I not see him, but I had to make do with minimal messaging to keep in touch with him at all. Even phone catch-ups seemed impossible to arrange. Ben hardly seemed available to me anymore, either physically or emotionally.

Consequently, I was spending my birthday with Mum, Dad, my brother and sister-in-law and their kids. We were going to my brother's house for a family Sunday roast, and I was looking forward to it. Sunday, at home, a family day. I knew Ben nipped out first thing to get the papers, so I was hoping for a quick call or voicemail. In fact, I had hoped he would make a special effort for my birthday, as things had been so difficult and tense for the last few months. Maybe even a surprise visit with a bunch of flowers… although, in reality, I knew this would never happen.

I checked my phone as soon as I woke up. There was the usual good morning message from Ben. It was a nice message. "Happy birthday – have a really lovely day xx". Nothing wrong with that. Except we had been in love with each other for two years now. I had received more emotional, heartfelt messages from some of my colleagues and acquaintances. Would it have killed him to say that he loved me and wished he could be with me? Maybe an extra kiss, a promise of a nice day out together soon or even a surprise gift?

I remembered the CD collection from last year. I thought about the way I had made his birthday special a few months before. Nothing extravagant, but I had phoned him, made him a special lunch as soon as he could come over. I had given him a particular book I knew he wanted, then out of print, so I had to search for it and order it especially. I gave him a funny mug for work and wrote him a sweet, romantic song all about us when we were younger. He had loved it and said he felt indulged and spoilt. I blinked back the tears and told myself it didn't matter. Birthdays were just another day, and Ben had a lot on his plate, as usual. But it was another chink in our relationship, another dent in my feelings, another ache in my heart.

I had a lovely day with my family, I really did. Mum made a cake for me covered in pink icing sugar, graced with pretty flowers and butterflies. I was given roses, chocolates, perfume, a plant for the flat and a new sweater. Thoughtful gifts and gestures, the sort of things people do when they care and want to show it.

I thought how much you were wanting that day, Ben, lacking in thought and gesture. I felt I was coming to know you better and I didn't like it, not really. You had changed, and your true colours were emerging. But I did not want to leave the love story we, or perhaps I, had created.

Next time I saw you I paid for lunch again. I made a joke that I was a little overwhelmed at the effort you had put into my birthday. You looked uncomfortable and hurriedly bought me a couple of CDs from a nearby record store. They didn't have much of a selection, but you managed to dig out something I might like. Not much thought really, but I said it didn't matter that you had forgotten to get me anything. I didn't want to make a fuss or for you to know how hurt I felt. And I didn't want to upset you or our day together.

I lied because it did matter. It really did.

I had hardly seen Ben for months, due to work and family commitments. If I got upset or merely said I missed him, he became irritated and annoyed and even more distant towards me. I felt like a nag, so I tried not to say anything about how I felt. But then everything seemed to boil up.

I'd end up either growing increasingly fed up with his neglect of me and not particularly wanting to talk to him at all, or I would pick at him and prick him for any kind of response. Even an angry response was better than nothing. Childish really, but this happens when the rules of a relationship seem to have changed, without either of you having said so.

Last and least, that's how I was beginning to feel. Last and least. Because it was Ben first, then his work, then his sad, dependent little family and then, just maybe, there was a tiny fragment left for Delphy Rose.

Delphy, his besotted secret lover, whom he professed to have always loved, yet was slowly destroying with his disregard and indifference.

Reg pulls pints at The Blackbird as it all kicks off

One surprising thing about Suzie and her cousin Becky was that they came from a large, religiously devout family who belonged to a local quasi-cult. I say surprising, because the girls did not exactly live a clean-living, religious life based on any kind of scripture. At eighteen, Becky regularly boasted about her voracious appetite for sex which she satisfied fully with whoever and whenever she saw fit. Both girls were in the pub and drunk most weekends. Suzie was only sixteen but looked old enough to get away with drinking in the local pubs and, in any case, underage drinking was much more relaxed in the eighties.

Suzie's father was quite high up in their extremist religious movement, so he must have been horrified by his rebellious daughter. Suzie certainly kicked back at all the rules and restrictions enforced upon her throughout her strict childhood.

One Tuesday night, it really did kick off. Becky had started seeing Richie, so the cousins became connected to the band again, which I was not terribly happy about. They were silly, attention-seeking little girls and proved too much of a distraction to their in-lust boyfriends. They started coming along to rehearsal at one point, but Ian and I both quickly stopped this. We paid for two hours' practice time on a Thursday night for the hall of a local social club and I was determined that we made the most of that time.

When Suzie and Becky started turning up, they were in and out with drinks, encouraged longer fag breaks for the smokers of the band, Richie and Ben, funnily enough, and were generally annoying. We would try to have a serious discussion about a new number, whilst Becky was hanging off Richie's neck and Suzie was sat on Ben's lap.

Enough was enough – the cousins were banned from rehearsals and that was that. Obviously, I was not overly popular with either of them, as they knew I had been the most vociferous. Ian was, as ever, laid-back, quiet and not liking confrontation. But he did back me up when I raised it at the band meeting.

So, Suzie and Becky were banned from the band, although they turned up at gigs, of course. Again, they were not allowed on stage and had to keep a distance from their blokes before and during the performance. They could hang off their necks, snog and lap curl as much as they wished, off stage, and once we had finished performing.

So, Tuesday night. We were playing at The Blackbird again. A good venue, plenty of space, good atmosphere and a friendly, musically minded landlord who made us feel welcome. And he always threw in a few free drinks at the end if we stayed for a chat with him – which we did, of course. Never could resist a free drink. He didn't charge us anything to play either.

No tickets, just whoever turned up, and we always brought in a good crowd which upped his takings on a normally quiet midweek evening.

We were doing a soundcheck when Ian nudged me. *Oh God, no drama please*, I thought.

Sheena had turned up. Sheena was Richie's old girlfriend. He'd dumped her for Becky. She always was a lovely looking girl, quiet, didn't say much, some would say boring. I quite liked Sheena and she thought the world of Richie. She had been pretty cut up when they finished. We'd had a few chats since, but she realised that I was in a bit of an awkward position as a band member, so our friendship was limited. I gave her a smile and she waved back.

Richie was looking as if he would rather be at the dentist's having a root canal. One thing I have learnt is that most blokes, particularly ex-boyfriends who dump you, hate being made to face the music. They hate to be confronted and publicly embarrassed. I'm not sure Richie ended it that well – that's if you ever can when someone else is involved; you've already moved on, and the other person has not.

Sheena stood there just watching the band for most of the gig. I have to say she looked stunning. Not sure what the point of her theatrical presence was – maybe she wanted to remind Richie of what he had given up; maybe it was an act of defiance towards Becky. But when the cousins arrived, she just stood, looking at them. She stood there, on her own, in her black leather trousers, bright red cowl-necked sweater and slash of matching red lipstick.

She looked absolutely knockout. She had a new short, spiky haircut and big gold hoops and an air of menace and defiance about her.

'It's going to kick off and Reg will never let us play in his pub again,' I whispered to Ian.

'Don't worry, it won't,' Ian assured me, ever the optimist.

He walked over to Sheena; they seemed to exchange a few pleasantries and he bought her a vodka and lime. She drank up, listened to a couple of numbers, then walked out with her head held high. One thing about Ian, he was a natural pacifier and good at keeping everything calm.

'What did you say to her?' I asked.

'Not much; I think she just wanted to make a point.'

Not sure what that point was, but I admired that shy, normally quiet girl's attitude. I think the point was, *I can come and go if I please; I don't feel uncomfortable and I'm still fantastic.* In other words, *fuck the pair of you!* Point very well made, Sheena. My estimation of her went right up that evening. Last time I heard, she'd married a roofer; they had five kids and were very happy together. Good for her.

Once Sheena had left, I could relax into my performance a bit more. I was halfway through "Talk To me, Don't Talk To Me" when two middle-aged men came storming through the front door of the pub, red-faced and shouting. I had no idea who they were and what was going on.

All I could hear was, 'Work of the Devil! Work of the Devil! You're all going to Hell! Hell for the lot of you!'

Blimey, I didn't think our music was *that* bad.

The next minute, Suzie and Becky were practically dragged out of the pub, screaming.

'Get off, Dad – we're entitled to enjoy ourselves – get off, you're embarrassing us!'

There was no violence, but the girls nevertheless made a hasty exit with the two dads who were determined to keep them away from the temptation, danger and sheer corruption of The Thistles. The weird thing was that throughout the entire drama, we all continued singing and playing, whilst the audience looked over, and then they carried on too, drinking, swaying, dancing. Friendly landlord Reg looked up briefly, shook his head and continued to pull pints.

Apparently, it was a fairly regular occurrence in the local pubs – the kidnapping of wayward teenage girls by their religious extremist dads. Suzie and Becky's family put up with a limited amount of hedonism and devilry, but it had to be limited to the weekends. Weekdays were about school, study and Church meetings. Any attempts to escape backfired, and the girls were publicly humiliated.

I noticed that Ben and Richie did not come to the rescue of their two naughty maidens. The dads were both builders, big and brawny and both boys were rock star slim. They focused hard on their instruments, kept their heads down and pretended not to notice whilst their girlfriends were being hijacked by the Dad Squad.

I only wished that Sheena had stayed on for another drink. She would have loved it.

Small love

I guess I thought you'd love me more
But early on you kept us small
As time went on and I went deep
I could feel you keep your distance

In absences, I wept for you
And all because you kept us small.

It could have been a great love
A meeting of minds
That had the makings
Of a true connection

I longed for your voice, your touch
But you decided to keep us small.

Twin flames,
We sparked off each other
Also sat quietly content.
The perfect fit

It seemed just right.
But you decided to love small.

That early sparkle
That little flame
Through flood and fire
You said you'd crawl

A long time waiting, longing
But you just had to keep us small.

It was Saturday morning. I used to love the weekends. Loved spending time on my own in my comfy little flat. I enjoyed having a boyfriend, but I was never sad when I was single. I would have lain in until about eight, then walked to my keep-fit class. After a quick tidy and general clean around the flat, I would put on comfy, weekend slouchy jeans and a sweater, treat myself to lunch and a hot chocolate at my local café.

After a leisurely flick through the Saturday papers, I would stroll around the street market buying fresh fruit and vegetables and chat to the local stallholders. Back at the flat, I would make a huge fresh fruit salad that I could dig into for a few days, and maybe a vegetarian curry or chilli for dinner that evening. Always enjoyed eating meat-free a couple of days a week. Music on in the background, relaxed and perfectly content. I used to enjoy being happy and at peace in my own little bubble.

I would usually do a bit of marking for an hour or so, or maybe some preparation for the following week's teaching, whilst dinner was simmering. Then I generally either went out for a drink with a few friends, maybe out on a date before I had started seeing Ben, or sometimes I would have a friend over. We would share the curry and go out for a couple of drinks, listen to a band or maybe go clubbing. If I had no plans to meet anyone, I was happy to spend my Saturday evening alone. Nice long, hot bath, face pack, glass of wine, good film and another lie-in to look forward to. Bliss.

Busy, satisfied, content. That was the old me.

In other words, I was doing quite nicely before you came along.

I knew the score when we met. He was married, but not married. But he *was* married, and he was not going to leave Jenny anytime soon, if at all. And I would not ask him. He told me that he gave what he could to our relationship. But there we were, still meeting secretly, and I had to ask myself – *Where was this all going?*

If I was truthful with myself, Ben's marriage seemed so lacking and stagnant and we seemed so right together that I thought we might, just might, have a happy ending. Like other couples sometimes did in those circumstances. Those times when a relationship goes stale and becomes a convenient, but tired-out social and financial construct. And then... BOOM! Along comes that special someone... right out of the blue.

Somebody who feels so right, a much better fit and suddenly it's time to wake up! Come out of the fog of worn-out matrimony and into the light of a brand-new chapter. A fabulous, hopefully final, chapter of happiness, passion and fun. A relationship based on those all-important ingredients of friendship and love but also physical attraction, sex, excitement and occasional fireworks! Not one centred on hanging onto a commitment that has become mere dry duty and dependency.

Saturdays were no longer so happy.

I tried my best to carry on with life, but weekends became a long stretch when I could not see or be with you. In fact, we had not spoken properly for weeks again. You were always so busy with work which seemed to demand more and more of your time and energy. When it wasn't work, it was your small family. Always some kind of problem with your wife and daughter. At least one of them constantly ill or requiring more and more of you. Jenny was often in bed with depression or headaches. Rachael's asthma seemed barely under control.

I had to wonder what made Jenny so unhappy. Could it be you? Was she unhappy because of your coldness towards her? You told me that she had suffered a breakdown five years previously. Was that when you stopped sleeping with her and she realised you no longer found her attractive, could not bear to touch her, lie close to her, or even kiss her properly?

I would look in the mirror at myself and wonder why you did not love me more. You sometimes said you loved me, but not as frequently as you did in the beginning. I usually said it first now. Calls continued to be infrequent and if I rang you, I was almost always automatically put through to voicemail. I felt uncomfortable ringing you during the week, as I did not like to intrude on your working day.

I looked in the mirror that Saturday evening and saw a kind, attractive face peer back at me. I had a petite, still slim figure, more gently rounded than when I was younger, but I was curvy and still cute. My long, black hair was glossy and thick, and when I wore it pulled back into a long ponytail, as I normally did for work, I still had a young girlish look. Just like when I sang in The Thistles. My eyes were bright blue and had a lively shine to them.

But I was sleeping with somebody else's husband, and I wondered if, despite the circumstances, that made me a bad person. Did one bad act make me a horrible person or did all the other good things I had done in my life somehow override the fact that I was sleeping with another woman's husband? I wasn't sure about that one.

When I looked in the mirror, really looked, I didn't appear any different. I was not gleeful; I was not gloating; nor was I bitter. I felt no malice towards Jenny. It seemed as if the marriage had broken down long ago, so I believed that I had done no further damage. I was respectful of boundaries and tried to be undemanding. But really, there were limits to my patience and the lack of freedom in my relationship with Ben was beginning to stifle and suffocate me.

The problem was, I was not only sleeping with Ben, I was also very much in love with him. At the start, we seemed to be equally emotionally invested. We were both as fully committed as we could be, given the limitations. We each expressed our importance to one another so that the many compromises and sacrifices were worth the effort.

But I was beginning to feel that things had changed. Or he had changed. Or maybe I had? Perhaps I expected too much? I tried to talk to Ben and told him how I felt. He seemed to listen, but nothing really altered. Any changes only lasted for a short while. He was not totally negligent – I would not have stood for that. And he was not nasty nor emotionally abusive, of course not.

But the rules seemed to be *his* rules. He set the rules of when we could talk, how long we talked for, when we could see each other. The gaps, the silences, the absences were due to Ben and his complicated life. His work, his family, his inability to make space and time for me were closing in on *us*.

And yet Ben did not seem at all bothered by the huge amount of time we were apart. He did not seem worried that we rarely talked properly because he was too busy and that the time was never right for him. Ben was able to distance himself in a way that I could not. And it was this ability to detach and his seeming indifference towards me that caused me so much pain and made me unhappy. Yet it continued.

I put on some make-up and smarter clothes. I wore my tight black jeans, a bright blue silky shirt, black ankle boots and my black leather jacket. I had washed my hair, so I wore it loose and chose some nice silver jewellery. I looked in the full-length mirror in the hall and felt pleased with my appearance.

A quick check of my phone just before walking out the door. There was a message from Ben, left later in the afternoon. He informed me that his favourite football team had lost, and he was in a bad mood. *Well, boo hoo! Not at all interested.* That's what I felt like typing but instead sent a sympathetic emoji and our customary two kisses. Didn't want to cross the line with too much emotion!

I tried not to think of him snuggled up on the sofa watching Saturday night TV with Jenny and Rachael. I turned off my phone, put it away for the evening and felt an instant sense of relief. Bloody phone. I would go to my local. There was always live music on at the weekend and I knew quite a few of the regulars.

I checked once again in the hall mirror and then added some eyeliner and a bright red lippy. Well, it was Saturday night.

John and Betsy

There was a record shop we used to visit occasionally, imaginatively named The Record Shop. It was owned by one of a kind, John. When asked why he did not think of a more original name, John shrugged and said he couldn't be bothered. Honest answer. The Record Shop was open for a few hours each day, more or less when it suited John, seven days a week. A small, independent music shop which stocked some fantastic material. John was a real character and a music obsessional. He used to play in a band called The Manky Cats and was also a talented illustrator.

He was usually sat behind the counter, surrounded by hundreds and thousands of records, music sheets and songbooks, listening to totally cool, eclectic music. He would often be sketching away, with a whisky bottle nearby. It could be eleven in the morning or four in the afternoon, and he would still be adding a drop of whisky to his mug of tea. Yet he never seemed at all tipsy, just used to it, we supposed.

He would sometimes draw caricatures of people browsing in his shop and handed them out as they walked by. If anyone offered to pay for it, he would shake his head and wave away the note with his hand. He didn't want their money.

'Take it – it's yours. I enjoyed drawing you,' he would say.

It was as if taking their money would take the pleasure out of the drawing and spoil his gift. Anyway, John was not particularly interested in money. His shop probably more or less covered his basic living costs, food for him and his little Jack Russell dog, Betsy, asleep in the basket behind the counter. Oh, and a couple of bottles of whisky each week and a few beers down the pub a few nights a week, of course.

Two blokes raided the shop once. Goodness knows why, as there was fuck all in the till, John told us sadly. He was a timid, good-hearted, insular old bloke and found it hard to comprehend the murkier side of life. The thugs gave him a few slaps before yelling at John to empty his till. Fortunately, Betsy woke up and surprised them. Angry little Betsy chased the cowards right out of the shop, yelling their heads off. Betsy was small, but fierce and a real ankle-biter. Concerned passers-by saw the almost comical sight of two toerags being chased out onto the pavement by sparky little Betsy and came into the shop to make sure John was OK.

'Shaken but not stirred,' he said a little weakly.

One lady made him a cuppa and asked where the sugar was. 'Good for shock,' she said.

'Only one thing I need, love,' said John, tapping the rim of his mug. It was duly topped with whisky. His tastes were known.

The police were called. No one had much of a description, until John started drawing and handed the policewoman a pretty accurate sketch.

'Blimey, you're good,' she said.

'Just observational,' he replied.

'No, you really *are* good,' she replied.

They tracked down the robbers and were able to secure a prosecution from the sketches and the testimonies of John and the passers-by. They both had records as long as their arms, so each did a spell inside. As John said, they went to prison for the chance of nicking fifty quid, because that was all he had in the till. Still, another two arseholes off the streets for a while at least, so job done, he winked. Good for John.

The power of an accurate eye, a sharp memory and steady hand. Despite glugging whisky all day, John was as sharp as a knife and a legend in our community. Well done to Betsy too, goes without saying.

Ben used to hang out in The Record Shop a lot. He was always drawn to slightly eccentric characters, who were on the edge of society, which was probably why he liked Keithie so much. Keithie frequently spent happy hours in Ben's back room, listening his way through his vast record collection. Unfortunately, this became a thing of the past, as Keithie became increasingly obsessed with getting his next fix.

One Sunday afternoon, l was cycling past the shop when I heard someone call out my name. It was Ben, poking his head out of the doorway, with a fag in his hand. You could smoke anywhere in the eighties. I put on my brakes and did an about-turn.

'Hey, what you up to, Delphy? Come on in, John's playing some of his band's old tracks. Pretty cool stuff, you'll love it.'

His band had a reggae vibe, and I did love it. John and Ben were having a cuppa (John's laced with his usual tipple) and a fag. The smoke from John's smelt distinctly herbal. I ended up staying for a few hours. I didn't often get the chance to spend time with Ben, as Ian was generally around, and it was a welcome break from study. At one point, John went upstairs for a while, and Ben and I sat chatting. It was nice, just the two of us, drinking tea, listening to music, flicking companionably through album covers. We were always comfortable in each other's company.

I could feel him looking at me when he thought I was not aware. He was obviously interested in me but never seemed able to tell me. I was his best mate's girlfriend, so there were boundaries, but even so... he would not get much encouragement from me even if he did fancy me like mad. I was brought up the old-fashioned way and liked a guy to make the first move.

John came down with his guitar and played a few tunes. Then Ben played on his spare guitar. I sang one of our songs and he strummed along.

'You kids – you're good,' said John, smiling through a fag.

'Well... we're never going to get on *Top of the Pops*.' I laughed.

I never could take a compliment.

'Sod *Top of the Pops*,' replied John. 'You shouldn't worry about being famous, making money or being like anyone else. Do your own thing; listen to lots of different types of music; read a lot; watch films; look around you and absorb all of life. Then go out there and create. Make music; write songs; find your own voice and be the very best you can. And enjoy it, just enjoy the music.'

And John was so right. As soon as you start creating for other people or trying to be like other people, you lose that special something that is uniquely yours, however fantastic or totally crap. It's yours. And you shouldn't let anyone take it away from you.

It was starting to get dark outside; I had homework to finish and school the next day. I said goodbye, and Ben offered to walk me home. I thanked him but said I had my bike and would be fine. I thought Ben looked a little disappointed, but I couldn't be sure. He was never one to give much away.

I cycled home in no time at all. I was hungry and needed to get my work done. I did not have the time to hang around in record shops chatting, especially with exams looming.

I had only gone out for some fresh air, but it was so nice to spend time doing nothing particularly productive. I had enjoyed chatting easily about music and the ways of the world with Ben and John.

I had that feeling once again that there was something between Ben and I. Or there could be if we gave it a chance. I often felt we would be better suited as a couple than Ian and I. More chemistry, more fire, but maybe too much?

Anyway, Ben had never asked me out and Ian did, so that was that. I had A levels to pass, a university place to win and a hell of a lot of work to do to achieve that. No time for romance; no time for complications. Ian loved me very much and everything was easy with him. No dramas, no hassles, no rows, no disappointments or let-downs. Ian was always there for me. It was as simple as that. Our relationship did not require effort or hard work, and it did not drain me. It just *was*.

When John died, it was discovered that his upstairs flat was filled with sketches and cartoons he had made over the many years he had worked in The Record Shop. He had never married, so it was left to his sister to sort out his belongings. She donated the whole of his artwork to the community of Cowlington. His paintings were given to schools, libraries, health clinics, community halls. The legacy of John was all over the town where he had been born, grown up, loved, lived and died.

His pictures lovingly and sometimes comically documented all the local, colourful characters who had walked into or past his shop over the years. People loved to spot themselves or someone they recognised, and John became even more of a local legend in death, as people often do. When I went to see a play at the local arts centre years later, I was thrilled to see a picture of me, Ian and Ben hanging in the waiting room. It was inscribed, *The young musicians who come and chat – members of The Thistles, great local band. Keep playing guys (and gal), John.*

I was tempted to enquire about buying it, but quite liked the idea of it hanging in a public space in Cowlington. Rock on The Thistles!

I still sometimes think of John. He did not lead a big life, nor a rich nor a glamorous one. But he was very much his own person and lived the life he wanted to live, surrounded by music, playing his guitar, drinking whisky tea and sketching portraits of everyday people, living everyday lives. A life lived small, simply and well.

Don't talk to me

It was one of those glorious summer days when I had to get out of the flat. I often went to Mum and Dad's for a roast on Sundays or we would all go round to Neil's. But Neil was at work all day and Sandy had taken the kids to see her parents. Mum and Dad had gone away to their caravan with a couple of friends. I was all on my lonesome, but I didn't mind.

I had spent most of Saturday marking and preparing for the final term of the year. Oh yes, the girl who always did her homework on Friday evening still liked to get ahead! Some things about me had not changed at least, I thought, with a wry smile. In other ways, I felt so very estranged from the young Delphy Rose.

Some days I was not sure who she was anymore.

I woke early at seven, threw on a sundress and strolled down to the beach for a morning swim. Feeling refreshed, I treated myself to a cappuccino and almond croissant at my usual café haunt. I took my time, flicked through the papers, had a chat with Di the owner and thought about what I would do for the rest of my day.

There was always a vintage market on the last Sunday of each month, so I decided to go back to the flat, shower and change and have a wander around the market. Then maybe a bike ride along the front and back onto the beach for a couple of hours to read and relax. I could pack a picnic tea and the rest of the bottle of wine I had opened on Friday evening. Sounded like a plan, I thought to myself happily, as I folded my newspapers, left a little tip and checked my phone.

It was the first time I had thought about the phone this morning which was a relief. I knew I was becoming too dependent on Ben's messages. His short, sparse messages with snapshots of his boring home life irritated me. It was nice to know he was thinking of me, but they were never enough. I really was not interested in hearing that he had made everyone a bacon sandwich for breakfast. Who cared really? I would much rather have heard something about how he was feeling... did he miss me perhaps? Did he wish he was with me?

But no, never anything cute, personal, nor remotely sexy from Ben. Nothing to intimate that we were lovers or even close good friends. Not his style, he was obviously far too deep and meaningful for all of that. *Too deep for a bit of fun*, I thought, with a sigh and a shrug. Apparently, details of Ben's journey into work, office politics and what his wife was cooking him for dinner were enough to keep me connected and close to him. I was not remotely interested in any of this of course.

I opened a message from him. "Good morning, what are you up to today?"

Do you really care? I thought resentfully. *And what does it have to do with you anyway?*

I would spend my day the way I wanted. I could not be bothered to answer, so I put my phone away in my bag.

You could keep, just as I was always waiting on hold and keeping warm for you.

The phone beeped again, as I was walking along the high street. There was a second message that I had missed.

"Just to let you know we are coming into Cowlington today – Jenny's brother is unwell, and she wanted to visit him. Sorry, only found out today. I doubt we will bump into each other, guessing you will be at your mum's or Neil's as usual on Sunday. But thought should give you the heads-up. You won't talk to me if you see me, will you? For the best of reasons of course xx".

And another one. Gosh, I was popular with Ben today.

"We are in the high street. Sorry, she got a headache and needed some pain relief from the chemist. Don't say hello if you see me, will you, please? Sorry xx".

There was always somebody ill in that family. I felt like messaging back:

"Yes, Ben, I'll come right over, wrap my arms around you and stick my tongue down your throat! I'm sure Jen won't mind!".

Did he think I was stupid or something?! I was tempted to ignore him and make him squirm for a bit, but I have always hated playing games in relationships. I texted flatly back, "Morning, got your messages xx".

I really could not be bothered. I kept it short and sweet to let him know I was not overly impressed. And then I saw them. Ben, Jenny and Rachael sitting together *en famille*, outside my second favourite café, looking all cosy and happy together, and just a few streets away from my flat. Could Jenny not have bought her pain pills from another chemist, and did they have to linger so close to *my part* of Cowlington? Did I need to have this happy family scenario foisted upon me like this? I was not about to go and sit on Ben's lap; of course I wasn't. But I was damned if I was going to turn around and take the long way back to my flat just for his convenience and comfort.

Besides, I needed to pick up bananas and milk from the 24/7. I walked past the happy family group, not too close, and on the other side of the road, trying hard not to look at them. I could feel that Ben spotted me. I felt sick and it hurt. My heart ached so much that it really did feel as if I was in physical pain. I wished I had walked the other way and picked up the milk later. I paid for my groceries with shaking hands, went home and looked at myself in the mirror. I looked pale and not quite myself.

The other woman, that's who I had become, and you had thrust that in my face by coming in so close with your family.

Ben made no mention of the incident when he messaged me later, but I knew he had seen me.

I talked to him about the incident when we next met up and told him how awful I had felt, seeing him like that with his wife and daughter. He sat there, silently, without expression. I asked him how he would feel if I had a husband or partner and he had seen us both sitting together, chatting and smiling. Or maybe how he would feel if I got back with Ian, and he saw us both having a coffee together.

'I would have walked the other way,' he said, with no emotion.

That was Ben and how he coped with life. He looked the other way, found another direction. He passed by anything that could be difficult or too demanding of him. He was emotionally lazy. He did not face up to harsh truths and hard decisions. Instead, he did all he could to avoid them and put his head in the sand. If he came up against an obstacle, he laid low, kept his head down and waited for the storm to pass. Or he walked away in another direction.

For all his talk, Ben did not face life head on. We were very different in that way.

Red handbag

I never did understand what you saw in Suzie. You said at the time she reminded you of me, but I could not see it. I was kind, attentive and affectionate towards Ian, respected him and did not play with people's hearts. Never have done. Suzie was young, silly, petulant. But you certainly got lost in her, didn't you? She had you on a string, had you running around all over the show. She broke your heart.

And I wondered whether I, and maybe other women, including your wife, paid the price for that early splintered heart when you gave and gave but ended up broken, hurt and humiliated?

Ben and Suzie continued to argue with each other and had multiple split-ups. During their many break-up periods, Suzie would delight in turning up to gigs with another bloke in tow. She would notice Ben looking over at her from the stage and snuggle into the unknowing guy, maybe plant a big kiss on his cheek or openly snog him in front of Ben. I could see Ben was seething. But by the next week, they were back together again, and it was Ben that Suzie was snogging. Suzie was fickle, knew Ben adored her and got a kick out of the excitement and attention when he came back to her again and again. And again.

To be fair, I thought you played your own games. Always flirty with the girls; if you knew Suzie was particularly jealous of someone, you would chat or linger at the bar a little longer than necessary. Not too long, nor too obviously, but just enough so that Suzie felt bothered by it. Maybe you never quite grew out of that need to game play and elicit a little jealousy or need for you. Perhaps you were even more insecure than I realised.

You were on another break-up from Suzie. Moping around, annoying the hell out of everyone. I sat and tried to talk with you, but I never did get much out of you when you were in that mood. You always clammed up when you were upset. It was something I remembered about you from our younger days. When you were hurt and vulnerable, you needed a lot of space and, for once, did not like to talk. I usually gave up trying to talk you round, but on this occasion I persisted.

It was a storm in a teacup, something out of nothing, Ben admitted. Now there was a surprise.

'Go and see her, for God's sake,' I urged.

We could not go on like this; his moods were driving everyone mad.

We were up in my bedroom, Ian, Ben and I, ostensibly talking through some new songs.

Instead, we were having a moan about a gig that had not gone well a few weeks ago. It was largely down to the poor management at the venue. Inadequate facilities, not enough room to put our equipment. We had asked for the largest room, which was spacious, clean and had good acoustics. It would have been perfect. When we arrived, we found out our room had been set up for a wedding, to be held the next day, and we had been relegated to the bar area. 'Sorry, last-minute booking, couldn't refuse.' Really? A sudden wedding booked for ninety guests?

The lying bastard.

If we hadn't sold so many tickets, we would have cancelled, but we felt we could not let our fans down. *Fans* was probably overstating it, but we had a regular crowd of friends and their acquaintances. We needed the money too. The Thistles account was running scarily low and, in any case, it would be too much hassle to issue refunds.

So, we gritted our teeth and went ahead with the gig. And it was crap. Our so-called *fans* bitched, complained and moaned all evening and rightly so. It was far too crammed; there was barely enough room to get to the bar; the beer was iffy, toilets got bunged up and the sound and lighting were rubbish.

We carried on regardless, like the troopers we were. At least we had the chance to sound out our new numbers to a proper audience. Not great feedback under those conditions, but hey, we learnt what we needed to work on. Play live and learn, as John always said, and we put the evening down to experience, even though it was not a good one. Luckily, most of the audience had heard us many times before and knew we could do better. They still heckled us, the buggers, but it could have been worse.

We were dissecting the whole sorry evening which was not exactly helping Ben's mood.

'Go and see her,' I urged Ben again.

If nothing else, his moping around was getting me down. Ben could be a miserable sod even when we were younger. He did not seem able to disguise his feelings and put on a bright face for the sake of everyone else. He gave us a resigned sort of half smile, picked up his leather jacket from my dressing table stool and walked out the door. Off he went for another lump of mental anguish, I thought. But he was not going to listen if I told him to dump her once and for all. He needed to keep going back until he finally realised for himself that she was not worth his love. Not even his friendship.

When he had gone, Ian and I smiled gently at each other, probably both thinking the same thoughts, as friends do. He sidled towards me for a kiss and cuddle. Ben wore both of us down from time to time. I confided that I was not sure if telling him to go and see Suzie was the best or worst advice I could have given. Ian moved in for a snog and we forgot about lovesick Ben.

An hour later, we heard the sound of my doorbell, and Ben came striding up the stairs. He looked pale and devastated.

We went downstairs to the kitchen, and I made us all a cuppa. Back in my room, I turned the music down and Ben told us what had happened. Suzie was not there when he went round to her house and the door was answered by her mum. Suzie's mum was lovely, nothing like her extremist, mad-as-a-box-of-frogs, religious zealot of a husband. I always thought her mum fancied Ben a bit, as middle-aged mums of girlfriends sometimes did. Nostalgia and yearning for youth and all that, I came to realise later in life.

Suzie was out, she said, at a friend's house doing homework. Yeah, right, probably round some squat, smoking weed or something, knowing young, not-so-innocent Suzie. Her mum told Ben she was on her own for the evening and wondered if he would like to come in for a cuppa? *Of course she did.* Ben very sensibly declined, knowing full well that, if caught in a clinch with the very amorous mum, her husband would, without doubt, have him crucified.

He walked straight round to Richie's instead.

Richie answered the door and looked a bit startled. His parents were out, and the music was on good and loud. He took his time answering, and Ben saw him run down the stairs through the small pane of glass in the front door.

Richie looked as if he had just tumbled out of bed, bare-chested, hurriedly-pulled-on, not-quite-zipped-up jeans, belt hanging. Slightly distracted, hair tousled, looking as though he had been interrupted.

Richie had just got out of bed. And he had been interrupted.

'Who are you with, Richie?' asked Ben.

'No one, just listening to a bit of music on my own, mate.'

'Can I come in then?'

'Erm, I'm just about to have a bath.' Richie's eyes darted as he came out with the most pathetic excuse a guy could come up with.

'You're having a bath? Since when did a bloke make an evening of having a bath? That's the sort of thing my sister says. What, are you doing your hair and having a face pack whilst you're at it?' asked Ben, looking him straight in the eyes.

'Course not, don't be daft.' Richie laughed but looked uncomfortable.

'Do you have something to tell me?' Ben asked plainly.

'No, just having a quiet one, as I said. Sorry, gotta go. Mum and Dad will be back, and I promised I would wash up.'

Again, not the best bloke excuse.

'Are you shagging Suzie, Richie?'

'What?'

'Well, it's pretty bloody obvious.'

Richie eyed the stairs nervously and decided to come clean.

'You heard her then, did you, mate? Sorry, Ben, she said you were over. Thought you wouldn't mind.'

'No, I didn't hear her actually. But I did notice her red handbag hanging on your stairs. It was a birthday present from me, so I should know it. And we were all sat in a pub together three days ago, so the term ex-girlfriend is a bit premature. Thanks mate – and you're welcome to her. I've had more than enough of her crap.'

And Ben walked away. As I said, my advice to him to go and see Suzie was both the best and the worst.

The pain of discovering how uncommitted and disloyal Suzie was towards him laid Ben low for many months. He certainly nursed a broken heart! But, one day, he finally saw her for what she was and could, at last, put a troubled, dysfunctional relationship to bed and move on. Unfortunately, it took another year or so for him to move on completely, but that was Ben and relationships. Just kept hanging on even when they should have been dead and buried.

Small boy

Small boy
Little hope
Grubby clothes
Short of soap

Dad's in jail
Mum's out all night
Toast for tea
Life's a fight

Just a child
Not much fun
Learns to hide
Wants to run

Given little
Needs more
Stops asking –
There's never more.

School had been quiet or quieter than usual. Jordan had not been in class for a couple of days. No word from home, so I planned to call his mum when I finished teaching, just to make sure everything was OK. Also, to remind her, yet again, that it was a legal requirement to inform us if Jordan was ill or unable to come into school on any one day and to give a reason.

It was a bright, fresh autumn day. The sun was shining, and we were able to go out into the school gardens in the afternoon. The school had developed some small allotments and each class had their own patch. The children loved it, watching their plants and vegetables grow, and maybe even picking and eating their own produce in the summer.

The allotments looked a little sad during the autumn, but there was still a bit of digging, weeding and tidying to do, and it was particularly good for my kids to get out in the fresh air, away from the confines of the classroom. They needed the structure and routine of class, but I liked to give them time outside as a treat. It was good for them to have space and run free a little.

The afternoon was warm enough to have the end-of-day story and song outside, so they all ran out bundled in coats, scarves and gloves. I kept spares for those who came to school without warm outer clothing. There were always a handful at least. We went out just in time to catch the last of the late autumn sunlight. A happy, peaceful time before they went off to their own homes – in the case of some of them, to goodness knows what.

Yet again, I had been summoned to the head's office at the end of the day. *She could have waited until the end of class instead of interrupting my flow,* I thought resentfully, as I nodded to the serious-faced messenger, fake smiled and tried to pick up my thread. It wasn't as if I was one to rush off at three-thirty. Teaching was not exactly a nine-to-five job for any of us.

I said goodbye to my class and waited until they were all collected or put into the various taxis and buses which took them home. There were fewer and fewer mainstream schools with special units like ours, thanks to yet more government cutbacks, so some of the children travelled quite a distance and had paid escorted transport to and from school. I tidied up for a bit before knocking on the headteacher's office door. *She can wait for a few moments*, I decided. When someone is on my back and overly demanding, I can get a bit petty, like most people.

Then I saw the look on the school secretary's face, and I knew it was something very, very bad.

Our esteemed head was sat at her desk, dressed up to the nines as usual, face covered in make-up, with thousands of pounds worth of glittering diamonds on every finger. Completely inappropriate for a headteacher of a state school, and particularly when dealing with the sorts of families we had to deal with, I thought, not for the first time.

A lot of the kids in my unit were on free school meals and some parents really struggled at the end of each week. I knew this because I had often given them quite a few weeks' grace to come up with money for school outings, etc. Some of the upper primary girls had started menstruating and were never sent into school with spare pads. Before the future state provision of free pads to schools, I always put a few extra packs into my shopping basket when I bought my own. The other teachers did the same. Period poverty amongst everything else. Poor loves, our children had so many needs. Unfortunately, our head was clueless and completely oblivious to most of them.

'Hello, Delphy, please do sit down,' she said gently.

She was being pleasant to me for once. It must be serious.

'There is no easy way to say this, but I am afraid I have some very bad news for you.'

Were there tears in her eyes as she spoke? I felt my throat tighten and my heart quicken. Please not Mum, please not Dad, please not my brother Neil, Sandy or the kids. And please not Ben.

It wasn't my family at all, thank God, nor anyone in my close friendship circle.

It was Jordan. The little kid who had caused me so much hassle all term, but who I knew was vulnerable and at risk. Jordan had not been at school that day because he had been truanting. He had been out and about on his bike, weaving in and out of alleyways, crossing busy roads, hanging around parks.

He had not taken his medication, and nobody had checked. He would have been agitated, anxious, distracted, probably high on sugar and Coca-Cola. He would not have been concentrating, looking or listening. 'He came from nowhere... he came from nowhere...' the distraught taxi driver said over and over.

He had not seen him coming as Jordan rode straight in front of him on a busy main road just off a roundabout. God knows what he was doing there.

He was killed outright, did not suffer. The tatty little rucksack he always carried was split open, throwing the contents across the street. The drugs he was carrying. We thought Jordan rode around the town aimlessly, but it turned out he was being used as a drugs carrier by one of his older brothers. His payment was fizzy drinks, chocolate and all the stuff that made him even more hyperactive and unable to concentrate. No wonder he was off the wall most of the time.

Nobody would suspect that an eleven-year-old boy with special needs was carrying drugs. He may have had a mouth like a sewer, but scruffy little Jordan posed no threat to anyone. That poor, ruffled-haired, confused kid, who was given so little care, was used as a drugs mule by his older arsehole of a brother, whom he adored and looked up to. It was scarcely believable.

I started crying. I was shocked, enraged and saddened by that little boy's pathetic life and the way he had been mistreated, neglected and abused by his own kin.

The head was surprisingly sympathetic. She put her sparkling hand on my shoulder and offered me a cup of tea and a lift home.

'It's OK; I'll be OK,' I mumbled, as I gulped back the tears and stumbled out of her office. I escaped into the ladies' loo for a real cry. Nothing worse than feeling vulnerable and accepting sympathy from someone you did not like nor respect and did not believe to be genuine.

I went out to the car and reached for my phone. I needed to talk to him. It went straight to voicemail. I tapped in a message.

"Sorry, I don't normally just ring, but can we please talk? Just for a few minutes".

You replied swiftly. "Can't, in a meeting. Sorry".

"Just five minutes, maybe when you finish?".

"No sorry, have to pick up Rachael from Girl Guides. Jenny ill again".

Sod Girl Guides, I thought. *I need you now*. Just this once. I needed to talk to my guy, the one who said I was the main woman in his life, if only circumstances were different.

I threw the phone back in my bag and drove home.

We had not spoken properly for a couple of weeks again and, to be honest, I was growing sick of it.

Because it was all about you. I felt increasingly that you called the shots, controlled our relationship, controlled me. It did not matter that I may want to talk to you or may have serious stuff going on in my life. We talked when you were able to, or when you wanted to talk. We talked when it was convenient and not at all difficult for you. I fitted in when you found time for me. I felt a need to stay connected with you, hear your voice, talk about our week and how we were feeling, how we were doing when we had not seen each other. You did not seem to share this need, and it really hurt me.

"Good morning, have a good day".

"You OK? Mental day, what you up to this evening?".

"Crashed out on sofa, Jenny having a bath, can't message for long".

"Night, night".

"Waiting for Rachael as usual, sorry she's out early, have to go now. Message you later".

"Traffic really bad, not able to stop and talk after all, sorry".

"Sorry, running late in office, can we chat another time instead?".

"Hey, have to go now, Jenny's just made tea".

Same old messages day in, day out. They were doing my head in, to be honest.

How about this for my day?

"Vulnerable nightmare of an eleven-year-old boy with special needs in my class, whom I have been trying to manage, educate and give some kind of care and direction, has been killed outright by a car. He was truanting and acting as a drugs mule for his scumbag of a brother. His mother is probably lying on her back somewhere in the town trying to score her rent. Night night. No kisses – you don't deserve my love".

I did not type this message, of course, but was very tempted.

I went to Mum's for the evening, had a good cry and a chat. A couple of hours later, I checked my phone. Nothing from Ben. I had spent so long constantly listening to his many woes and problems, around his job, his own health issues and stresses and his dysfunctional, ill family. So where was he when I needed someone to listen to me? Now I was the one who needed some TLC and where was he?

I switched off my phone and ran a bath. Fuck him. Fuck him and fuck Jordan's shit of a brother. That poor kid never stood a chance. I was so angry at the injustice of his life.

Next day, Saturday. It would be difficult, but not impossible, for Ben to call me at the weekend. I didn't expect much. Despite my better judgement, I flicked on my phone again.

"Hello, sorry about last night. Mental day, had to work late in the evening after picking up Rachael. Then Jenny had another headache. Still, nice relaxing day to look forward to. Have a lovely Saturday xx".

So that was it until Monday, I guessed. I was not going to ask to speak with you again. I thought you may have called me back last night or suggested we speak this morning when you went out to get the papers or some shopping. You did not consider that I may have an important reason for speaking to you or may need to talk something through. I always respected your space, your personal life, your work life. I played by the rules. But you did not stop to think that I may have needed you last night – and may still.

I should have answered Ben's message, but how on earth could I describe what had happened and how I felt in a text message? Communicating that huge event and the tidal wave of sadness I felt in a few lines of text would further degrade Jordan's life.

I switched off my phone again. Fuck him. I felt petty again. Ben was making me feel petty because he seemed incapable of thinking outside his own tiny world.

Besides, I had more important things to think about. On Monday, I needed to find a way to tell the class what had happened to their classmate. I also needed to think about what we could do as a school and a community to honour Jordan and his sad little life. Because it had to stand for something.

Joe's kebabs

We had played a gig at Candlelabra, not one of our usual venues. The place did not live up to its rather upper-class, glamorous name. A tatty set of rooms rented out for parties, gigs and the odd dance or keep-fit class. We were performing with The Splints, an unusual band made up of a bunch of arty geeks from the local FE college. Lead guitarist Richie's nan worked at Candelabra as a cleaner, so it cost us next to nothing. We had little else planned, so we thought we would give it a go.

It turned out OK really. We sold more tickets than we thought we would for a January gig and, as the room hire rate was next to nothing, we were easily quids in. We had heard The Splints a few times and they certainly had an eclectic sound. Bit of everything, really mixed it up. Rockabilly, rock and roll, bit of folk, bit of punk. They could do it all. And they wrote all their own material. The guys were all quiet and unassuming with distinctly arty images. They all wore make-up and hats. Lead singer, Jimmy, was dressed as a country gent or medical consultant (or something like that) in a waistcoat and bow tie. They knew their place as our support band and did not try to dominate or take over so were easy to play with.

Quite a few of their college friends and family members came along which made for a varied, random audience.

Grandparents mixed in with punks and art students – interesting crowd, I liked it. One of the grandads did a bit of pogoing at one point, and Jimmy's mum and dad did a mean twist to one of their rockabilly numbers.

Richie's nan kept going around clearing glasses and picking up empty crisp packets and binning them. She certainly took her cleaning responsibilities seriously and never seemed to be off duty. Still, it made clearing up a lot easier at the end and she even swept the floor for us before she left. What an angel.

We had the venue until twelve and it was a Saturday night, no school or work the next day, so we all stayed behind afterwards and had a few beers and a chat. We didn't always hit it off with our support bands and weren't sure we would get on with those guys, so it was a nice surprise that we did and a relaxing end to a good evening.

And then those fatal words.

'Anyone fancy a kebab?'

We were on the north side of town which meant only one place. *Joe's.*

Joe's was a legendary kebab van that everyone gravitated to when they had had a few. It was one of those rituals, those habits you just kept repeating, even though you knew it was rarely a good idea.

I groaned and shook my head. 'No, not tonight, guys. I've got to write an essay tomorrow and I can't face a morning on the loo,' I pleaded.

'That was only once, Delphy, don't be a *girl*. Come on, you know you love a kebab after a few beers.'

I often felt they forgot I *was* a girl. But, as usual, I caved in for fear of missing out on something. Yes, ridiculous, but I was young and foolhardy. And off we headed for Joe's.

'Hello, my good friends. Still pretending to be rock stars? What can I get you then?'

Joe was horrendous. He looked even greasier than the grey dripping carcass from which he carved thick, disgustingly smelling slices of fatty meat. Fag hanging from his rubber-lipped mouth, and occasionally dropping into the food, he burped and swore his way around his van. He stood confident and proud in his stained white vest underneath a dirty apron with *I'm Sexy* emblazoned across it.

Joe had one of those floppy, greasy fringes, never seemed to wash his hair, was always unshaven and seemed to be constantly picking his ears or rubbing his nose. And no one wore hygiene catering gloves in those days. Filthy nails that I tried hard never to look at, and every finger covered in huge, gold sovereign rings, probably harbouring an entire zoo of bacteria.

Only problem was his kebabs were *delicious*. Particularly after a few drinks, which is when we always turned up at Joe's. And one of the few places still open, back in the days when there weren't dozens of late-night eateries and cafés all over the town.

'Ketchup with that?' Joe picked up a huge bottle of ketchup, with strings of dried drips that looked as if they had been hanging there for centuries. Then picked up a filthy rag and rubbed it across the counter in a highly theatrical manner. Despite the dramatics, it was left no cleaner.

'What do you want, love?' asked Joe, fag ash dropping over the kebab he was wrapping for Ian. Poor Ian.

'Erm…'

The problem was the chest hair. Joe had a rug of curly, black chest hair which also looked despicably greasy. And it had been found in his kebabs. At least we assumed it was chest hair, but God only knew. The problem with chest hairs is that they look remarkably like pubic hairs, which is exactly what we picked up on one night when Richie found he had been chewing on one. And Ian. And Ben. Those hairs made frequent appearances and could be very easily disguised by Joe's special spicy sauce. It was his very own special recipe, apparently. *Heavens.*

'Shuddup with your yapping, Sadie. She goes on at me more than my bloody missus!'

I could never believe that someone was married to slobby Joe, but hey, love is blind, so they say. You couldn't help who you fell in love with. I'm sure Joe had some attractive points, he just kept them under wraps. Sadie was the little black poodle Joe had recently acquired, and he kept her in the van with him when he worked late evenings. He looked after her well; in fact, that was just the way he talked. I was just never sure about the health, safety and legal side of having a dog in a food van.

But yes, his kebabs were tasty and, despite the fags, the dog, the nose-wiping, arse-scratching and fallen hairs, they were pretty much irresistible once you'd had a few pints inside you, and everyone around you was chomping on one.

'You can share mine if you like, Delph?'

That was Ben, never a big eater.

I hesitated, then took a bite with Ben looking on. Where was the harm if I took just the one bite? A big bite mind, they were bloody delicious. He never gave away the recipe for his special spicy sauce which was probably just as well. Exactly the right amount of grease, tasteless meat, spicy sauce and crunchy cabbage to fill a gap at that time of night. Mmmm, then… *oh my God, oh my God!* Something not quite right in my mouth. I spat out, horrified. A big, black… whole bunch of… hairs…?!

I stared, totally horrified at the chest rug ahead of me, as Joe happily sloshed his sauce, and thought of something much, much worse and then looked at the little black poodle... oh God! Please, oh please, surely not dog hair?! What had I put in my mouth? I held it gingerly in my fingers.

It was... it was... a moustache. A whole black moustache.

Ben and Ian were absolutely pissing themselves laughing, and Joe was looking on totally ignorant. Ben had paid a visit to the local joke shop, We Got Ya!, a couple of days ago with their little prank in mind. It had all been planned – once he took the kebab from Joe, he quickly placed the little black moustache deep in the sauce, at the far end of the meaty offering. This was the end he offered to me, because he knew I was fussy and would not eat straight after someone else's bite.

Ben knew I was almost sick every time someone had a hairy kebab, curtesy of Joe, and could not resist the practical joke. Ian was in on it too, of course. The bastards! I whacked the pair of them around the head and yelled at them before I stomped off.

They were both doubled up with laughter.

'You're just too easy to wind up, fusspot Delphy!' grinned Ben.

Joe, totally oblivious, called after us. 'Another one going spare if you want it, gang?'

Complete with special spicy sauce and curly hair. Mmm... delicious!

'See you next time then?'

Joe could be quite needy for a big, lairy guy. But let's face it, he probably would see us again. It was cheap and usually the only place open when you were pissed and desperately hungry for some grease to soak up the beer. I ignored Ian and

Ben all the way home, just to teach them a lesson. I didn't mind a laugh and was never precious about being the only girl in The Thistles, but I always have had a thing about hairs in food. Quite naturally and understandably so. Plus, I took quite a bit of banter from the guys, and it was good to put them in their place once in a while.

Exam results

Results day and I did well! Didn't quite get into Leeds, but I got good passes in English, History and Art and, after a few calls, secured a place at a London poly studying Combined Arts to include English Lit, Dance, Drama, Music and Art. The poly offered a Voice and Songwriting module, and I could go on to do a teaching certificate at the end of my degree.

I had been looking forward to going up North, but the idea of London was exciting and a great place to see bands, and maybe perform a little myself, so I was pleased and excited!

I thought it was sweet when you phoned my home to see how I had done. You phoned before Ian actually. You were certainly in a funny mood for a while before I left. Many years later you said you didn't want me to go away and that you really missed me when I left Cowlington. If only you had told me how you felt then!

Maybe things would have turned out differently. But Ben, being Ben, kept his feelings to himself and ended up marrying someone he did not really love enough. Instead of waiting for *The Real Thing*. Instead of gathering up his feelings, taking a deep breath and approaching me.

The next few weeks were a scurry of applying for my student grant, buying books for preparatory reading and getting together bits and pieces for my new lodgings. I would be living in a shared flat with three other girls on the course, two in their second year, which was useful as they would know the ropes. I was nervous but looking forward to resuming my studies, excited about the experience of moving away from home for the first time and could hardly believe I would be living in London.

I had applied for a transfer with Woollies, not expecting much. I was only a Saturday girl, after all. However, I had worked there since I was fifteen; they knew I was reliable, pleasant and hard-working, so it was worth a try. I could do with the extra cash, and it saved me having to find a job when I was trying to settle into my studies, getting to know the poly and finding my way around London.

On my last day at work, the manager called me into his office. They had a job for me in one of their large stores very close to the polytechnic. I could easily walk or cycle through the park if I took my bike, so that was handy. They also gave me a *Goodbye and Good Luck* card, plus a voucher for fifty quid. For Woollies of course, but much appreciated thanks! And a big box of chocolates. Woohoo! I was bored stiff of working there really, but they were a nice crowd and, quite unexpectedly, I felt a little sad about leaving.

Of course, the real farewell celebration was a night out with the crazy women who still worked there, and who had first introduced me to all the local lively pubs, bars and live bands when I started working at Woollies. We changed into our going-out gear after work and did our make-up in the loos, whilst cracking open a bottle of Liebfraumilch in preparation for a big night out.

A couple of hours later, we were in the middle of town on a major pub crawl and then dancing ourselves dizzy at a local club into the early hours. We had a ball, good clean fun, no blokes involved, just seven ladies out on the town, and we all slept at Ruby's afterwards. They were terrific company; we always had a hoot; and it was the kind of night out that I would miss.

I knew Ian was a bit upset that I had spent my last Saturday night out with my workmates, rather than with him and the gang, but at that age I didn't worry too much about pleasing other people. I was quite selfish really, when I was younger, and generally did what *I* wanted to do. I was independent, free-spirited and far less loaded down with baggage and responsibility than in later years. I feared being judged less. I liked Ian very much, felt attracted to him, enjoyed his company and the sex was good, but I always knew he was not the love of my life. I thought the right guy for me, my soulmate, my life partner, would come along later in life, but that was not my focus at eighteen. And rightly so.

A few more days at home, time to see Ian, Penny, and other old schoolfriends, then one more band rehearsal before The Thistles appointed a replacement singer. Then I would be on the train to London. The start of a new life and a new adventure. I could not wait. I would miss everyone, felt apprehensive and nervous about living away from home for the first time but also knew that this was something I had to do.

I needed to escape the comfort and confines of family, friends and Cowlington. I knew I needed to leave home to fully experience the next stage of my life.

Presence

I feel your presence
Here in my arms
Pressed close to me
I feel your firmness
Pressed against me
As we kiss, as we caress

It's the presence of you
That I hold in my heart
It's the presence of you
The way you were at the start

The presence of you
Before you turned hard
Before I realised
Your cold, brittle heart

I hold the presence of you
The way we were at the start.

You came to visit me shortly after you heard about Jordan, spent
most of the day with me. It was half-term so a real privilege to see
you on a weekday. It was so nice to hug and be held. Good to talk

with someone who knew me like no other. I read out my testimony to you and you thought it was lovely.

We met again at the end of the week. You had a tooth filled the previous day and it hurt a lot, so I drove over to you, as Jenny had taken Rachael to visit her cousins for a couple of days. You were not good with physical pain, you said. You were worried about it falling out. Work was getting you down. Someone had upset you again. You were very low, in pain, even began to weep a little. Silent droplets trickled down your cheeks as you spoke. I had rarely seen a man cry and it alarmed me a little. I held your hand and tried to soothe you. I spent most of the afternoon listening to all your work problems and how you felt about the difficulties you faced. I used your bathroom and when I came back, I found you scribbling on the bottom of Jordan's revised testimony. I had brought it over to read it through with you before the funeral.

'You may like to add this to what you say,' you suggested.

When I left, I thought about the time we had spent together that afternoon. A little boy I had known, taught and supported had just recently been killed in horrendous circumstances.

But somehow, Ben had turned this around, so it was all about him. I was still in a state of shock and grief. Those feelings do not go away in a few days. I drove home and thought how very weak, self-centred and pathetic Ben could be at times. I was beginning to feel that the man I loved was very different from the Ben I remembered all those years ago.

You were not the man I imagined you would grow into.

I could not help but wonder what had happened to the caring, kind young man I used to know, who had always seemed so empathetic. I now began to wonder if I was involved with some kind of narcissist.

The ravages and losses in life had changed you, I reflected. The stresses of work and the disappointment of your marriage had brought out the worst in you, I felt.

We had so little opportunities like the one we had today. But you had not wanted to make love or even cuddle up with me. You needed space, you said, when you felt like this and chastised me when I came onto you a little. You told me you were not in the mood to have sex. How about making love then? I felt like asking.

But I said nothing.

I felt drained as I drove home and disappointed by Ben's behaviour. I would have liked to have lost myself in him that day. I wanted to feel close and connected to the man I loved and take away some of the pain I felt, if only for a few hours. It did not take much to bring him down, I concluded. I would have hoped for more resilience.

I was not sure how much I liked the new you. You used to have more heart.

Where was my Ben and who had he become? I reread my testimony and rubbed out the comments he had added at the end.

You did not know Jordan; you had no right to add anything to the script. Just for once, it was not all about you.

Away to study

One of the cool things about being away from home was receiving letters from Ian, friends and my family. Even people I thought of as mere acquaintances seemed to enjoy receiving my letters, and I enjoyed getting them back, particularly in those first homesick weeks.

Dear Babyshakes(!)

Missing you sooooooo much baby. Reallyyyyyyy look forward to our phone chats on Wednesday nights. Thought you seemed a bit down last time... are you sure you're OK? Some of your tutors sound really UNCOOL, but sure you'll do well. If they give you a hard time, let me know... I'll come and sort them out for you. (Actually, you would probably do a better job yourself. You and your fiery temper, my little firecracker. It's one of the things I love about you!)

Not much news really. Ben is still moping over Suzie (he really should get over it). Went for a drink with him last night and bumped into Tom and Darren. They all said how much they missed you. Made me feel kind of proud that you mean a lot to them, too. (But we all know I'm your special one, of course!)

Band is going well. Our new lead singer, Squirrel (I know, we still don't know his real name), is a bit of a twat really but seems to be fitting in quite well. You're probably thinking there's a reason for that and smiling right now! I think he may be seeing Penny. She was back from art school last weekend, and they seemed very "into" each other. Watch this space… will keep you posted, of course.

Squirrel has a good voice, obviously nowhere near as good as yours, my dearest love, but then I am very much biased. (Seriously, you really do have a much better voice than his.)

He is no good at writing songs either. Maybe you could send some on to us, if you ever have time to write a few ditties in-between doing all that coursework and dealing with moody tutors?? You do write a good lyric. We miss that.

Work is work, pretty busy, but still boring. Very tired of all the driving and wish I could change to a more local office, but hey, when you're working in the dynamic and extremely vital industry of life insurance, you have to keep in the cut and thrust of things, Baby!

Had a bit of a cold last week, feeling better today. Not much else to say really. Except… cannot wait for you to come home for your Reading Week. I am looking forward to treating you like a princess for your birthday. Also, it's nearly our anniversary, Babycakes, so I'm going to get you something special. I thought we could go somewhere nice to eat, just the two of us. (We always seem to go out with a crowd, and I kind of want you all to myself pleeeeeeeeeease…)

Anyway, call me on Wednesday, as usual (are we boring??) and I'll ring you back like I always do. Mum is fine with it – she knows I miss you and we need to catch up. But I'll give her a bit extra towards the phone bill, so we can relax and have a nice long chat.

Love you always and forever, Babycheeks

Ian

Xxxxxxxxxxxxxxx……………………(infinity)

Ben's letters were short, succinct, funny.

Dear Delphy,

Well, my dear, it certainly is quieter in town without you. Must admit I found it quite emotional when we had our last night out all together. But was also a bit annoyed that I wasn't invited to your final Saturday night out with the Woollies crowd. I bet it was a steaming night – you know I hate missing out on legendary nights in town.

Ian is fine, obviously missing you, and a bit stressed with all the travelling he is doing with this new job, but we are looking after him, so don't you worry.

Band is going well. Penny's replacement Squirrel (what sort of a fucking name is that?) thinks he is really cool but isn't a bad singer. (Actually, he is really quite cool, but don't say I said so. I'm really rather jealous, if I'm honest.) And if I say "really" one more time… I will throw all my Stranglers records in the bin.

I hear you are house sharing with some other lovely females. Are they fit? If so, can you please tell them about your very handsome and funny, single, ultra-cool friend… no, not fucking Squirrel!!! Me, of course. Please introduce me when I come and visit you which I hope to do one day. (Well, that's if Ian lets me – he can be quite possessive of you.)

Have to go now. In my bedroom listening to The Doors (you really should get into them, you know) and Mum is calling me down for my tea. Sometimes I feel that a cool rock star, such as myself, should move out into digs or something, but where would I get hotel service and luxury for a tenner a week? And you really can't beat my mum's Sunday roast, followed by her legendary fruit crumble and custard. Best meal of the week.

Look after yourself, Trouble.

Ian says you are back home for Reading Week or some such shit?

Take good care and whatever you do/don't do – stay cool.

Ben

PS So over Suzie.

PPS Why do you need a whole week off to read? Yet another example of the ease of student life. (Some of us have to work for a bloody living… moan, moan.)

PPPS I'm probably just jealous. Personally, I'd love a week off. I might even read a book.

Penny visits

Once I was settled, student life in London was great fun. I got a full grant due to Dad losing his job, like so many others in Cowlington in the eighties. He was OK though, did a few odd jobs here and there, got some shifts in a warehouse, and then Mum signed up at our local tech, trained to be a chiropodist and did quite well at it. So, they were alright. 'If it doesn't kill you, it makes you stronger' was the motto my dad lived by. Unemployment in his forties was not going to get him down – he just picked himself up, did what he could to bring in some money and tightened his belt.

I learnt a lot of my determination and resilience from my dad. 'Life doesn't get you down if you don't let it. Put a smile on your face; pretend you're OK; and one day you will be.'

My dad the survivor.

Penny came to visit for the weekend, a few weeks before I went home for Reading Week. She was enjoying art school but was a little lonely, I think. It was hard being away from your close friends, your family and everything you'd always known. It could be stressful having to fit in and mix with other students from very different backgrounds and regions.

Penny and I had an absolute ball that weekend. We heard a student band play at the polytechnic bar, then went out on the town to a few pubs and clubs. We talked about the guys for a bit. I had to confess that I did not really miss Ian as much as he seemed to miss me. And I was noticing that he made such a big thing about everything! Getting a new job and having to travel some distance to work seemed to be a highly stressful, mammoth-sized challenge for him. *Big deal*, I thought, most people who wanted to get on in life realised that they may have to move away or be slightly inconvenienced at some stage! Unless they were happy with a job behind the counter of the corner shop or in the local supermarket or factory, that is. I knew I would not be.

I was beginning to realise that we were very different people who wanted different things from life. Ian obviously missed me a lot but hadn't even suggested coming to visit, although I was not too far away. He was fun to hang out with; I enjoyed his company, but our expectations were very different. I could be anxious and feel scared of doing new things, but I was thirsty for new experiences and, as much as I loved and admired my parents, I did not want their limited lives.

I wanted more. Didn't know what exactly, but I knew I was longing for new experiences.

I wanted to travel, live in different places, try a variety of different jobs, until I found something I loved doing and was really good at. Whenever I heard someone boasting proudly that they had worked in the same job, same institution, or same company for forty-odd years, I felt my heart sink and my mood drop. I knew that would not be me.

Chatting with Penny, I began to understand that I was beginning to move on and away from Ian. It was a shame because he was a lovely guy who thought the world of me. So annoying that feelings don't often match up at the same time! Life would be a lot easier.

Shiver, then whisper

I shiver and then whisper
I can barely form the words
This moment I scarcely conceive
Because one day you were here
And the next you had to leave.

Not sure what the point was
Of your few and fragile years
You were loud and you were difficult
Yet scared and full of fears.

So life goes on without you,
But with me, you've left your mark
There's a space that feels quite empty
Death is final, cold and stark.

I did not say these words at Jordan's funeral.

Instead, I talked about what a fun character he was. How he loved to hear a story when he could sit still for more than five minutes – that raised a smile and a few laughs. How he loved garden time – when he wasn't pushing some poor kid's face in the dirt or throwing stones at the classroom windows. I didn't say that either, of course. How he loved to sing...

and... and... how much I enjoyed teaching him. Lied again — he was a pain in the arse most days.

I had wanted so much to be able to stand there and say something coherent, meaningful and nice. And preferably without bursting into floods of tears.

But I had to ask myself — what was the point of Jordan's short life? This is what I really wanted to say out loud at that sham of a funeral. Jordan was unloved and so became hard *to* love, or even *like* at times. His quality of life was zero; he had no joy, motivation or spirit and was raised in an environment of selfish, unkind neglect.

But I played my part well. Fortunately, teaching gives you a few acting skills that helped me give that little boy a half-decent send-off.

I appreciated your text message, wishing me well and saying you knew I would read beautifully, but so wished you could have been there with me. Or at least come round to the flat later to hold me, stroke my hair and kiss me, so that I felt the world was not so unfair and harsh. But, of course, you couldn't, and I would never have asked you. I did try hard not to make additional demands on you, knowing you already had so many at work and at home.

The testimony went well. My TA, Marion, the one Jordan regularly called a c★★★, read a lovely poem about some of us gracing our world for just a short while but experiencing and spreading so much joy and happiness during that time. The head even bestowed the day with a few words. She managed to sound quite genuine for once. *Miaow.* None of Jordan's family contributed anything. Quite frankly, I was surprised they turned up.

That was unfair — his mum was in bits, bless her. God knows where she was when the police finally got hold of her. Probably thought she was about to be banged up like Jordan's dad and kept her head down for a few hours. Wherever she was, and whatever she was up to, she must have been feeling absolutely rotten that she was nowhere to be found, whilst her son lay dead on a mortuary slab, awaiting identification by his next of kin. I spoke with her a little and gave her a hug. She cried and thanked me for all I had done for her son.

I looked around at the masses of flowers sent to the crematorium in honour of Jordan. There was always a big reaction when a local child died. I tried not to feel bitter. We had to fight to get Jordan all kinds of extra help in class: behavioural therapy, speech and language therapy, one-to-one teaching assistant support. He nearly lost his free school meals allowance at one point. I looked at all the beautiful, expensive, but pointless, flowers and thought how much difference that money could have made to Jordan and to other kids at the school. Such a shame that a little lost boy, right at the bottom of the pile of society, had to die before he gained the attention and care he so badly needed.

I left with the feeling that we could all have done so much more.

I messaged you when I came out of the funeral. You replied later in the evening. Short, sparse messages. You were obviously watching TV with Jenny, or maybe had Rachael cuddled up with you. You were sympathetic, supportive in your own logical, matter-of-fact way. "Have a lovely evening, try to relax. Message you tomorrow".

I wished he had said "I love you, Delphy". It would have meant so much more. Or just offered to ring me tomorrow. But he didn't, and I was not going to ask him. *It's part of the game*, I thought. Must not show too much affection, need, love or ask for more. Must not upset the delicate balance of the extramarital relationship.

I worried that if asked for too much of him, he may resent me, assume I was becoming too demanding, perhaps think less of me for not being strong enough? I did not want him to feel bad, compromised, or put out in any way. I worried I would lose him if the relationship became too difficult, so I did all I could not to expect too much of him. If he said no to me, he couldn't, he was busy, or it was difficult (why was everything always so *difficult* in his life?), I tried not to feel slighted, insignificant or demeaned. But I generally did feel that way. It was a very unsatisfying arrangement and probably another good reason not to have a relationship with a married man who was not really married. But was.

I took his advice, had a warm bath, then an early night. Next day, a message from Ben on his way to work. It was nice enough, short but sweet. "Hey, morning. Off to work, hope you feel better today". I knew I would probably get another message at about six in the evening.

"Hey, finished now. Good day?" And then maybe another one later in the evening... "Home now".

Then I would message back, maybe no more evening communication. I would find a reply to my "Goodnight" text in the morning, as I tended to go to bed earlier than him. And so, it went on, sometimes for weeks, when we could not meet and did not have a chance to talk properly. He was too busy, and there was no time. Ben's idea of a relationship, but not mine. Maybe there was a reason his wife was so unhappy? Maybe this was just not enough for me?

So why, oh why, could I not walk away from him?

Fluffy cowl neck,
leather mini skirt

Dearest loved one,

How ya doing? You sounded a bit low on the phone on Thursday? I hope you're not getting homesick and missing your very cool boyfriend too much (that's me, of course). But can quite understand if you do!! We are kind of a cute couple. It's been an eventful couple of days. Suzie is now officially going out with Dillon who is, as usual, behaving like a total idiot. They keep turning up at the pub and generally seem to be trying to wind up Ben who, as you can guess, is on the verge of going completely mental at them both. Not sure why they can't just go off together and keep out of his way. Suzie seems to enjoy making Ben jealous – probably enjoying the attention of two blokes fighting over her.

Silly little girl.

Anyway, they turned up at the gig last night. Suzie had on a tight, cream, fluffy cowl neck jumper and a leather miniskirt. She had obviously made a big effort. They kept laughing together loudly and looking over at Ben. It was a repeat performance of the time before, you remember? When they were snogging all over the place and seemed to be doing everything they could to annoy him?

Ben looked as if he was about to explode but was trying his best to concentrate on the gig. Then, all of a sudden, her dad and grandad came bursting through the doors with a few other religious extremities! There was a massive row between them and Dillon; then Bob the landlord got involved. At one point Dillon smashed a glass and started threatening Suzie's dad. It got really lairy! Anyway, no blood shed, but the police were called and Suzie's dad, grandad and Dillon were carted off to the station! The landlord barred them all but thankfully did not blame us. Good outcome! It's a cool little venue and we always do well there, as you know. And most importantly of all... they do a good pint of bitter.

Ben was laughing his head off when they were taken away by the police. So at least he was happier than he has been for a while and, thankfully, he stayed out of any trouble. We're thinking of putting a couple of useful people on the door next time we play anywhere – like Keithie (if he's not too stoned) and maybe Jimbo. We could give them free tickets and a pint. All this background aggro! Very disruptive to the creative vibe, man!! But also very rock and roll...

Oh, and Penny and Squirrel are now very definitely an item. Let's hope she goes gently with his nuts... ha ha, geddit!!

Yours everlastingly and lovingly,
Ian-babes xxxxxxxx... (infinite number).

Well, I was quite impressed by Ian's female fashion knowledge when I read that letter. Especially considering that he did not have a sister; his mum dressed like a granny; and I was his first real girlfriend. It was news to me that he even knew what a cowl neck was. Intriguing.

And I think he meant to say religious *extremists*, not extremities, bless him. It may have been a joke but probably wasn't. I did not pick him up on it, as I knew he was a little sensitive that I was studying for a degree, and he was not. You had to be quite careful when you were one of the minority in your group who went on to higher education. You could easily get a reputation for thinking you were too big for your boots and too good for Cowlington.

Squirrel and Penny? Wow! I would not have put those two together, but hey, I just hoped he looked after her and treated her right. Weird she didn't mention it to me when she came to stay for the weekend, but I knew she could be a dark horse. Hence "Thirty-Five-Year-Old Married Twat". I also knew that Penny was vulnerable underneath all the laddish bravado, so I always worried when she was involved romantically with anyone. Especially someone who was a bit of a "character" like Squirrel. Those types could be charismatic, but unreliable, and tended to hurt soft-hearted gals like Pen.

I loved to hear all the news but always felt a little left out after reading letters from home, so perhaps I missed Cowlington more than I realised. Yet going back and giving up was never an option, so I put away my letters and carried on with my coursework, my new friends and my new life. My next letter from Pen told me all about getting off with Squirrel when she was home last time – she went home too often, I thought – and how they were now an item.

Oh, for the days before texting and messaging. You had to wait much longer for news, and nothing was so instant. It was all less urgent, less immediate and somehow more special. Fewer opportunities for misunderstandings, miscommunications and messing up.

Life seemed simpler.

Busy, always busy

"Hey, how are you? Busy, busy, never seems to let up much these days. Sorry not much contact, just the way it is. Just stopped off to have a coffee, then off to work. Hope you have a good day xx".

A message from Ben. He had time to stop off for a coffee. Could he not have pressed call and given me a surprise "good morning"? I would have loved it.

We had not seen each other for five weeks, not spoken on the phone for more than a fortnight. I wondered if he had noticed how long it had been. I did not want to ask him to call me, as if I was desperate and could not cope without him. Besides, he should want and need to speak to me, however busy he was. Once a week, that's all I wanted, and I had asked him several times now. He seemed to listen, but only after I had been upset about his apparent neglect of me and of us. We did not seem to be equally invested in our relationship.

I had not said much to him, as I had not had the chance. I had not been great, not really.

Not since Jordan's death. It was a shock to all of us. There was also now an inquiry into the school. There were several questions around the way in which we handled Jordan's constant truanting. The head went on sick leave with depression. I knew she was not up to the job, did not have the required experience, but I actually felt sorry for her. Our jobs were hard – the kids we taught, or tried to teach, were extremely challenging, and there was sod all support from home most of the time.

Like Jordan's mum, many of the parents were struggling to keep their own heads above water, so the kids received minimum attention. And those kids needed so much attention and care. Teaching children with learning difficulties and mental health issues, with all their frustrations, anger and, at times, a lack of even average parenting, could crack the most able.

Some of our parents were not the most able and were hard to communicate with. They did not, or could not, listen. Several had similar problems to their children but had never been properly diagnosed. It was all so sad and hard to deal with at the best of times. And this was the very worst of times. A small child had been killed in a dreadful accident that would not have happened if he had been under the school's care. Under my care. It was almost impossible not to feel overwhelmed.

On top of Jordan's death, the subsequent investigations and a substitute headteacher who was clearly not capable of leading and supporting us through this ordeal, I had an ever-increasing workload. Resources had been cut again, yet expectations continued to rise. State education is always hard and special education even harder.

I had always loved my job but was beginning to wonder if I could carry on like this for the rest of my working life. I was not feeling well. I was exhausted but not sleeping well. My appetite was poor, and I could not shift a cold that had been dragging on since Jordan's funeral. I felt physically and emotionally run-down, and also worried that I was experiencing mild depression.

I always used to feel better when I talked with you, but you never seemed to be there now. Always rushing off somewhere, never time to talk properly. I had spent so long listening to your problems and trying to support you, but you were not there when I needed you. Maybe that was the problem? You didn't want me to need you. I was drowning, but you did not want to know that. You wanted strong, fun, fantasy Delphy. The Delphy you thought you used to know. Not the real, fragile thing.

And I wanted the Ben I used to know. The kind, gentle Ben who thought the world of me and would do anything for me. The guy I used to argue with but secretly admired, respected and maybe loved too.

I now wondered whether you loved me at all. Or even liked me when I was weak like this. I was worried that I was going to lose you but could not help asking you for more. You were giving me less and less. It made me demand more. You gave me even less, and the distance between us became greater.

The classic demand and withdrawal traits and psychological tension of a dysfunctional relationship, often based on earlier experiences. I had read all about these relationships and never thought I had attachment issues. I felt trapped in a treadmill of disappointment and dissatisfaction.

And it was killing us. More significantly, it was killing me.

Penny and banker

Penny visited me again. She was homesick but did not want to keep going back home, as it would worry her dad and gran. She came to see me instead. I never minded that she came so frequently. It was always good to see Pen. She told me that although she had got off with Squirrel when she last went home, she was not really that interested in him, and they were not an item anymore. He was too nice and a bit boring. Typical Penny!

She was closer to home than me, so often popped back for the weekend. I personally thought she would do better if she stayed put at college for a bit longer, but I knew she still missed her mum and was more vulnerable than she appeared. I kept my thoughts to myself and always enjoyed her visits.

We were sitting in my bedroom, eating cornflakes with cold milk, sprinkled with sugar. We had no money, as usual, and we were bored.

'Let's go busking,' suggested Penny randomly.

'OK... have you ever busked before?'

'No, but we have good enough voices, and I've read poems in shopping centres and stuff, so it can't be that difficult. Come on, it'll be a laugh, and we might make enough money to have a good night out.'

Penny had brought along her guitar, and it was true that we could both sing, so why not?

We made a flask of coffee, put on our coats, scarves and gloves. It was freezing outside. We found a good, sheltered spot, set up and began to entertain passers-by.

It was exceptionally cold, and we felt a little self-conscious at first, but we soon got going.

We did OK. Penny's hat started filling up nicely, and we even made a new friend, the homeless guy pitched up in the nearby shop doorway. He was very encouraging and our new biggest fan. Penny strummed along to a couple of her latest poems. None about abortion, periods or losing her virginity, thank goodness. We sang a duet that we wrote together the last time she visited. It was called "Fragments" and became one of my favourites. I sang some Thistles stuff, plus a few covers. After an hour or so, we were freezing cold, a bit fed up and filled with both sympathy and admiration for the homeless guy. It was extremely miserable hanging around outside in the cold. We decided it was time to head off back to my digs.

A couple of blokes had been watching us for a while. They strolled over as we were packing up. They were a few years older than us, both nice-looking and quite fanciable.

'Nice voices, girls. Fancy a drink?'

We looked at each other. It did not take much negotiating. I was still technically going out with Ian, but it was only a drink after all, and I had already decided I was going to end things with him next time I went back to Cowlington.

'Why not?' said Penny, a bit too eagerly, I thought. 'Give us ten minutes to pack up our gear.'

Penny counted our takings and looked over at Steve, our new best fan, who was bedding down uncomfortably for what we imagined would be another hard night. She looked at me with those big, soft eyes. *Go on then*, I nodded. She went and bought Steve a coffee and a sandwich, then shrugged and gave him the rest of the coins. No notes, perhaps not unsurprisingly. Big, warm-hearted Penny. That soft heart of hers meant she could be a pushover with blokes but also made her one of the kindest people I knew.

'Cold night, mate.'

Steve nodded and thanked her with an appreciative thumbs up.

'You two are great,' he told us. 'You're gonna be famous one day. You'll be on *Top of the Pops* singing with all the stars, you wait. I can see it now.'

Yeah right, Steve. Probably more chance of us flouncing around with Pan's People.

We knew our limitations.

We walked to a nearby bar with the two heart-throbs. They turned out to be good company. Paul (SBG – Super Brainy Guy) was at uni doing a PhD in something obscure and impressive sounding. Dan worked for a bank (BG – Banker Guy). Oh well, someone had to. I wasn't sure how Penny would take to a capitalist. She was turning out to be very communist since joining art college, but they seemed very attracted to each other. We had a few drinks, a bit of a laugh, then went for chips at our request. We liked to keep it simple. And we loved chips.

'Fancy coming back to mine for a coffee and listen to some music?' suggested SBG.

Penny was clearly besotted with Banker Guy (BG), so the answer was yes. Obviously.

As usual, I ended up chatting in the kitchen with the quiet one (SBG), whilst Penny was snogging on the settee with BG. I explained that I was currently in a relationship which was coming to an end. SBG was single and seemed to respect my honesty. We agreed to put things on hold and keep in touch until I had sorted things out with Ian. It was all very grown-up and civilised, I thought.

Retrospectively, he probably was just not that into me.

In truth, although it would have been nice to go on a date with someone new, I was looking forward to not seeing anyone properly for a while. I had been with Ian all through sixth form and wanted a bit of free time to myself. Time to do exactly as I pleased with no commitments.

No ties, no scheduled Wednesday evening phone chat and no frequent, time-consuming letter writing. Ian was sending me three letters a week, and I felt obliged to reply, despite not really having much to write and being busy with assignments. I knew he missed me, but it was all getting a bit claustrophobic.

I heard Penny ask where the bathroom was, then BG poked his head round the door.

'Alright if we use your bedroom, mate?'

I winced at the choice of the word *use*. It sounded cold and functional, but I could not think of an alternative way of asking. I felt sorry for Penny, for some reason, but reminded myself that she was not drunk, and it was her choice. I was not her mother.

SBG nodded blankly and made no comment.

We listened to giggles from Penny, the shutting of a door.

'He's married with a kid,' said SBG when they were out of earshot. 'Still puts it about quite a bit though.'

'Oh, does he?'

We had been here before.

'Where are you going?'

'Rescue my friend Pen.'

'What?'

'She's not as robust as she looks, and he should know better.'

I was not going through that again, and neither was Penny.

I took a deep breath and was just about to knock on the bedroom door when Penny rushed out, red-smudged lippy, panda eyes, hair all over the place.

'He's only bloody married!' she hissed.

'Really?'

'Yes. Married, but not married. You know the story.'

'Well, you certainly do.'

'Not falling for that again. And he's such a bloody capitalist – you should hear him! Bloody obsessed with dick-swinging and bonuses and all that bollocks. Come on, let's get out of here. I'm bored.'

Funny, quirky, wise Penny. She wasn't going to make that mistake again. She had learnt a lesson early and learnt it well. Years later, I wished I had.

As for SBG, never saw nor heard from him again. Can't say I was too bothered.

Little things

I used to love your laugh
And long to hear your voice
That slight husk
The little sniff on the phone
As you paused for thought.

That curling grin
The way your eyes
Became more blue
As we sat and talked
And talked and talked.

Your tightly mouthed kiss
Not generous
But just enough.
You were never going to give
Too much of yourself away, were you?

That honesty
The sense you needed to confess
Made you seem so vulnerable
At first, the real thing —
My hand in glove.

Like a little boy
Not quite grown up
And there was the problem
The little boy
Not yet grown up.

Too afraid to give too much
Not able to give in or compromise.
And so, I hold out, hold on tight
Wait for a chance, a change
A gap big enough to fit me in.

And then… and then
The laugh is no longer enough
The voice no longer captivates
The sniff that annoys.

It's the little things that lead us to love
And it's the little things that kill it.

It had been ages, but you invited me to meet you for a drink and a meal. It was a rush after work and I had to make excuses to get out of a meeting, but I charged home, made myself look pretty and ran for the train. You were held up. I stood around waiting for you in the cold for about half an hour. And then another half an hour. It wasn't your fault; you couldn't help it – meetings ran late. I did feel a little fed up, frequently waiting around for you, but pushed away those nagging thoughts. I was always the one who was inconvenienced, putting myself out, making allowances. Waiting, waiting, waiting and fitting in with you and your inflexible, restricted, difficult life.

As I was getting ready that evening, part of me wanted to cancel. I think I was getting to that point, at last, where

I realised this was going nowhere. But then that yearning would come back, the kiss, the hug, the holding of hands, that feeling we shared at the beginning. The fix, the emotional tug. I wanted my fix, my love drug, and so I ran for the train even though the logical part of me was warning me to stay clear. *This is not enough. You deserve more.* My inner voice was yelling at me, but I declined to listen.

But he loves me, he really does. Doesn't he? Or is he flattered, trying to recapture the past, making up for the gap in his life? Can't really be bothered and does not have the time, but he's addicted too. He needs his love fix. Just occasionally, and maybe less than me, but he needs it too. Drip, drip, it's exciting, makes him feel good, keeps him going. Drip, drip, can't quite give me up, even though this is no longer fun for either of us.

We met; we kissed; you apologised for being late (again). I smiled and said I understood. We walked to our usual pub, and you bought the drinks. You weren't drinking as you were driving and had an early start tomorrow, you said.

We sat down in the centre of the crowded pub.

'Can I ask you to do something for me?' You leant towards me and asked so nicely.

'Of course, anything for you, darling.'

I looked up at you lovingly, pleased to help you. I loved doing anything I could to support you, to try to make you happy. It made me feel close to you and special.

It was your wife's birthday and you had forgotten. You wanted to cut short our date so that you could get home early and give her a present and her card. That was what you wanted me to do for you that evening. You suggested that I accompanied you part of the way home so that we could chat a little longer, and then I could take another, less direct train home that night on my own. My instinct

*was to throw my drink straight in your face and afterwards I wished
I had. I felt so very disappointed in you and your lack of regard for
me that evening. I was also taken aback that you asked me out and
somehow had not realised that it was your wife's birthday. How
thoughtless and careless were you?*

I felt even more hurt as I was still waiting for a proper
acknowledgement of my own birthday. We had been seeing
each other for a long time and, as far as I was concerned, a
text on my birthday was not enough. I was hoping that we
were going to do something special that evening. Something
to make up for all the let-downs I had put up with over the
last six months or so. But no, nothing. He seemed to have
forgotten or, even worse, not even considered doing something
significant to celebrate my special day. However, I was expected
to accommodate belated plans for Jenny's birthday.

I was beginning to feel like a mere colleague, an
acquaintance, someone for him to talk with occasionally and
have the odd day out with when it was convenient and not
too much trouble. I felt that Ben treated me less and less like
someone he was in an intimate relationship with, his close
friend, his lover. I was beginning to feel shabby, the other
woman, his bit on the side.

*I did all I could to make you feel loved, supported and
important. At that moment, I utterly despised you for making me
feel like a cliché in the fiction section of a women's magazine.*

*I did not throw that glass of wine. Instead, I held onto my
dignity. I drank the wine straight down, put on my coat and scarf
and picked up my bag.*

*I walked out of the pub and away from you. How dare you
make me feel like this? You seemed like a stranger that evening,
someone I did not know at all. But maybe I had been blind to your
true colours. Maybe I had not seen the other side of you.*

Wedding gig

I was home for the holidays and singing with The Thistles again. Ian had seemed so thrilled to see me when I came back. I could not bring myself to end things with him. Squirrel had seemingly disappeared off the face of the earth, or at least the face of Cowlington.

Penny was away in the New Forest, staying with her sister in their caravan for most of the summer.

We were asked to play at the wedding of Gary, older brother of our keyboard player, Andy. Didn't expect us to do it for free, but could do it cheap? Yes, of course we could. We always enjoyed playing live. It was a swiftly arranged affair, as his bride-to-be, Joanne, was five and a half months' pregnant. Apparently, Joanne didn't realise she was pregnant initially. She had started a new job in a cake factory and thought she put on a bit of "cake weight". She had obviously been enjoying the cakes so much that she hadn't realised she had missed four or five periods also.

I glanced over at her as we were setting up. She wore a desperate wedding dress. A big, sturdy girl, the dress clung far too tightly in all the wrong places. It had a train with a short skirt at the front exposing most of her fleshy thighs, and this was pulled up even higher by her not insignificant bump. And it was very orange. I had never seen an orange wedding dress before and never have since. Probably for good reason.

She looked like a bloated satsuma. Her enormous, pregnant boobs were hanging out all over the show and she wore bright orange flowers in her auburn hair. Of course, I told her she looked just lovely, hypocrite that I was.

'How long have Joanne and your brother been going out?' I asked Andy.

'Five and half months,' he replied.

'Oh.'

Not much to say to that.

The venue was a shabby, dusty community hall, festooned with a few tired-looking balloons and some plastic blue and yellow flowers that looked like they'd been nicked from the local church. Or maybe even the cemetery up the road. Looking around at their guests, that was not an improbable assumption. We were told that we couldn't share in the buffet as "numbers were tightly catered for". We looked over at the trestle table covered in a flowery plastic tablecloth that looked as if it had seen better days. And needed a good wipe. A few plates of white bread sandwiches, bits of dry quiche and some manky-looking sausage rolls. A classy affair then. I was glad I'd eaten earlier.

They even had a raffle at the interval. Never seen that at a wedding before either. They said the money was going to a charitable cause. Charitable cause, my arse. *Gary's pocket most probably*, I thought, very uncharitably. I always thought he was a bit of a shyster and was glad we were charging something for the gig. Poor Andy looked embarrassed. He wasn't anything like his family. A quiet guy, unassuming, happy to keep in the background. And an amazing musician. We were lucky to have him. But his family left a lot to be desired.

The happy couple danced together to their signatory romantic song. They hadn't been together long enough to have their own smoochy song, so the DJ picked one for them. They seemed awkward and ill at ease with each other and clearly did not look right together.

After the raffle everyone was invited to do a bit of barn dancing. Joanne's family were mad keen barn dancers apparently. I have always loathed that kind of thing, but soon we were all pulled from the stage and made to join in the fun and games. Five punk band kids dressed in leather, tartan and tie-dye barn dancing with a load of losers.

Thank God no one we respected saw us. Andy looked as if he could die. He knew we would take the piss out of him for weeks after this. He would never live it down. He was nicknamed "Barnet" for about two years after that night. We didn't forget things easily in The Thistles.

One funny thing to note was that the best man was in fact a best *woman*. She was the groom's best friend, apparently. Dressed in a badly fitting man's suit, the best woman spent most of the evening hanging out with, and dancing with, the new groom. His bride, the lovely Joanne, sat with her many sisters and cousins, telling them all about her new kitchen lino, festoon blinds and how awful her piles were now she was pregnant. I swear she got an Argos catalogue out at one point. That was in between having a fag and a swig from a bottle of white wine. And yes, she swigged straight from *the bottle*. Nothing like a classy bride and health-conscious, pregnant mum-to-be.

We did a set of our own songs, then a few covers, plus a couple of rock and roll numbers that had been requested. I'm not sure what they made of us, but most of the guests were pretty pissed, so they were all up dancing anyway. When we finished, the DJ took over and they seemed a lot happier with seventies disco hits.

'Get me out of here,' said Ben in disgust.

He was totally "uncooled" by the whole wedding, he said later. Barn dancing, corned beef sandwiches, rubbish music – he had a point.

I went out towards the kitchen to wash my hands and get a glass of water. The ladies' loos were swimming in *something*, full of girls laughing raucously and smoking. I couldn't face them. I opened the kitchen door and was instead confronted with Newly Married Groom of the Century, Gary. With his tongue stuck down the throat of… yes, of course, his best friend and best woman. And whatever else she was to him.

'Oh… sorry!' I backed out as quickly as I had barged in.

'It's not what it looks like…' stuttered Gary, as he came after me, quickly looking over his shoulder to check no one else had seen.

'I honestly don't care, Gary,' I replied truthfully. 'But I would like to know why on earth you are going through with this charade? It's the rest of your life, you know? She may be pregnant with your baby, but she's bloody awful and you obviously don't love her. And even you can do better than that.'

'Thanks… I think,' Gary replied, simultaneously offended and complimented.

I was never anything less than completely honest when I was younger. Those less fond of me sometimes described me as extremely tactless and occasionally rude.

'Sorry, but—'

'Look, it's about doing the right thing,' explained Gary with a certain amount of pride, visibly standing straighter. 'She's pregnant; I've got my responsibilities now.'

I looked at him, not knowing what to say. And it was none of my business anyway.

'You won't say anything to her, Delphy, will you? And not to Andy or any of the others…?'

He looked worried and not without reason. Not that many marriages break up within six or seven hours of tying the knot.

'No, of course not. I don't even know Joanne and, as I keep saying, it really is nothing to do with me.'

Gary looked relieved as I walked away.

I felt sorry for the pair of them. What a start to married life! From what I had seen, marriage seemed difficult enough, without any extra pressures and complications. Mum and Dad mostly seemed happy enough with each other, particularly when Dad was earning good money, the house was in a good state, and there were no real problems, health, kids or otherwise. But they had their ups and downs like most people. I guessed a lacklustre marriage could become utterly miserable when under pressure.

Gary thought he was doing the right thing by marrying his pregnant, very recent girlfriend. He was willing to change his life path for that noble reason, despite snogging another girl in the kitchen on the very evening of his wedding. That night, I think I realised that relationships were often not black and white at all. There were many shades of neutral.

I also realised that satsuma orange is a drastically unbecoming colour for a bridal gown.

I would have given Gary and Joanne six months, but believe it or not, they lasted for twenty years until Joanne left him for another woman. Poor Gary was heartbroken.

And it wasn't his best woman/best friend. That would have been a tidy ending.

Your game

Just someone I used to love
Just someone I used to know
Someone I thought was my world
But now I can't afford to let it show
Can't show how much I care or feel
In case it's seen as weakness
Have to stay on the outside
Because you won't let me in.

So now you're just someone
Someone I used to love
I don't know you after all
Seen a different side of you
Or perhaps a side I tried to ignore.
But I can't ignore it anymore
You're no good for me
You're not right for me
You don't make me happy

It's a game now between us
A competition, who loves least
And who endures most
And I will always be the loser.

Because I can't compartmentalise
Can't keep my feelings in a box
Can't shut my love down
When it's inconvenient for you.

But I don't know you anymore
And I don't want to love you.

And are you really the winner
Because I can't play your game?

I should have carried on walking away from you that evening. The evening when you wanted to drag me across town with you, in a pathetic attempt to spend more time with me, whilst still getting home to give Jenny her card and present. Lucky Jenny! She got more than I did, that meagre birthday text message still rankled, but I felt pity for her.

She had a husband who arranged to meet another woman on her birthday, which he had obviously forgotten about, and then attempted to keep two women "happy" by being with them both on the same evening. It was *the stuff of sitcom* and could have been funny, if it was not so pathetic, hurtful and frankly disrespectful of both myself and Jenny.

Talk about wanting to have his cake and eat it. Our relationship was beginning to unravel. That was obvious to me that night. Our *special something* was evaporating in the mist of lies, broken promises and sheer emotional cowardice. I was complicit in this tangled little web of deceit and so could hardly complain when I was also treated in a second-rate, hand-me-down fashion.

I complained, of course I did. I went back and really let him have it. But I did go back. And I saw him standing there, looking so lost and helpless, that I felt sorry again. Sorry for him, sorry for his sad, unsatisfying marriage, sorry for the trap he found himself in, and sorry for what we were becoming. I took him in my arms, we kissed away the hurt and talked and talked.

He said he was sorry; he knew he was wrong but had made plans to see me before realising it was Jenny's birthday. I was still not sure how he could forget his wife's birthday. But when love takes over, it's surprising how far logic goes out of the window. He was just trying to do the right thing, he explained. By both of us. However, I was beginning to realise that *doing the right thing* was not always possible in secret, stolen relationships.

And so, we were on again. For now. I sat on the train home, in an empty carriage, feeling uncomfortable and lonely. I felt as if I had lost something. I realised, much later on, that it was my sense of dignity, decency and self-respect. Part of me was relieved that I had not lost Ben. Part of me knew I should have carried on walking. Because that was the way to freedom and to finding myself again. Getting back to Delphy and all that she represented at her very best. The relationship was not fulfilling. I was having to compromise too much and accept far too little. I was enmeshed, and could not quite let go, despite knowing that it was in my best interests to leave and get on with my life. Properly, truthfully and completely.

I should have been living a better life. I should not have been living a half-life, waiting in the shadows, accepting a twilight love that was not destined to see the light of day.

The dream

Dreaming of you
Dreaming of grey
Of rain of drizzle
Days and nights of tears
Waking and missing you
Lonely and longing
Feeling desolate and knowing
That it's not the same for you.

And that's what destroys love. It's not always lies nor hatred necessarily, not even violence. It may be carelessness, thoughtlessness and indifference. It's the feeling that you are not important; you do not figure. That's what kills love ultimately. It's sometimes what you don't do, rather than what you do. You don't say you love me; you don't send that card; you don't make time to call; you don't listen to what I have said. Or you pretend to listen, seem to do all these things and you say that you care, but your actions do not reflect your supposed feelings.

I had yet another dream about Ben. I was not sleeping all that well. In my dream we were young once more. At the start of the dream, I was walking along a pavement, in the dark and alone. It was a wintry Sunday evening. I hated Sunday evenings when I was growing up. I always felt low.

In those days, the entire day was boring and dreary, as far as I was concerned.

Dull, tedious Sunday school, no shops open, nothing on TV, curtains drawn at four in the afternoon during autumn and winter months. I felt so trapped and restrained, getting my stuff ready for school the next day, my dad moaning about going to work on Monday, Mum scrabbling around for dinner money and panicking that the uniforms weren't dry. Seeing all those little socks and knickers and grey uniforms drying by the fire made me feel even sadder for some reason. It all seemed so drab and predictably monotonous.

So, in my dream, I was a teenager again, eighteen or nineteen years old, just walking along. And I was missing Ben. I had not seen him for a while; we had not talked; maybe we had quarrelled or upset each other. I did not know. I just knew that I was sad and missed him.

Suddenly, I realised that I could go and see Ben. I was able to knock on his door and see him at that very moment. I would be welcomed by his mum, who would ask me in. And there he would be, probably in his front room playing records, smoking a cigarette. I could speak with him freely and immediately, when and where I wished. I felt liberated and lifted by this thought.

We were young and carefree again. Ben was not married, and he was still living at home with his parents. There were no restrictions, no constraints, no Jenny, no Rachael. No one keeping him imprisoned with their invisible walls of need and dependency. The weather was miserable, drizzly, cold, misty. It felt like November or January, a grey dog of an evening. The dream was in black and white, like an old, British, kitchen-sink drama. Pretty grim. No American technicolour; no pizzazz; no loud, optimistic background music. It was all gloom and working-class doom. Realism. No happy ending.

But as I was walking along towards Ben, as I often did in those frequent dreams, something stopped me. There was always something to prevent me from reaching him. I either changed my mind and went another way, or I was taken off track in my path to him. This time it was my nan, who had passed away many years ago. I was walking towards the road where Ben lived and there she was. My deceased nan, wearing a good, thick, 1950's check coat and a headscarf, in true working-class filmic fashion. Just as she looked in some of the old family photos I had seen.

My nan suddenly appeared from nowhere and redirected me, persuading me to come with her instead. And I placed my arm in my nan's, and I walked away from Ben. I walked away with my nan by my side.

When I woke up, it all felt very real. I lay in my warm, cosy bed and slowly dissected my dream. It seemed that Nan came to protect me and guide me towards a safer, steadier path. The grey, the cold and the drizzle represented to me the misery of being with a cold-hearted, brittle man who had nothing to give me anymore and who could not give me, or maybe anyone, his wholehearted love.

In my dream, my nan prevented me from going back to you with your dreary life centred around work, work and more work and barely any room left for fun, excitement or happiness. Or even love. My head-scarfed nan pointed me in a different direction and my dream told me to stay away from you and to not go back. My nan was looking out for me and took me away from something potentially harmful. She was trying to take me away from you.

I realised then that you were not my destiny. I was not meant to be with you after all, and I would not ultimately be happy with you. It was a mistake to think we could make this arrangement work. I was not even sure you had the ability to love when someone loved you too. When I thought back to your past relationships, and remembered the stories you had shared with me, I realised that you were the sort of man who could only love the unattainable, the uncommitted and the unreachable.

Maybe you were the true romantic underneath your cold exterior. I did not know. I was a teacher, not a psychologist. But I did know even then that to really love someone took courage and a boldness that I did not believe you had. You cannot love fully if you are scared. And you were scared.

Maybe it takes a dream to wake from a dream? I felt I was finally waking from my dream version of Ben, and of us, and beginning to need something real and with more substance.

I felt I was going through another stage of growing up. A transition. I was growing and evolving into a stronger, more self-assured woman who would not make do and settle for less or enough. I realised with a jolt that this fractured, crumbling relationship was beneath me.

I needed to find my way out before I totally lost myself and became a wisp of the woman I should have been at that stage of my life. I needed to be strong to become stronger.

I needed to get away from you.

Three flat caps and two dogs

The Thistles had a gig booked during Reading Week and invited me to sing with them. The new lead singer was away again, and Penny was working flat out on an art project. I still had not finished with Ian. He was so excited to see me again, and I realised that I was pleased to see him too.

He had taken a couple of days off work to spend some time with me, so I did not really have the heart to tell him I thought things were slipping away. And maybe they weren't, after all? We still enjoyed each other's company, talked, laughed, had good sex. Maybe it was just me, adjusting to life away from home and the new course. Maybe I was looking for something more that did not really exist? Perhaps good enough was well, enough, really.

The gig was at The New Tavern, which made a change from the more usual Ye Olde Taverne, and it was on the other side of town. We did not know the pub but were excited at the prospect of a Friday night booking. Generally, we were shoved into a quiet weekday slot. The landlord presumed he may as well have a few kids in, making a racket and bringing in extra punters, even if some of them were on lemonade, cola and crisps. Quite a few younger siblings and their friends came along to our performances at that stage. They gave our gigs a certain naïve, innocent air which I quite liked. They could also liven things up with their natural exuberance, lack of inhibitions and the pure excitement of being out for the evening in Cowlington.

The landlord of The New Tavern was Big Trev. Big Trev was a jolly sort of bloke who said he would pay us a flat rate, no tickets to be issued. He assured us he would fill the place with his regulars, all music lovers, and that Friday was always a lively, busy night. He did not want his pub totally overrun with kids, so definitely no tickets. He would sort us out with an audience.

As usual, we turned up nice and early to set up. We had not had time to check out the venue. It was all organised on the phone by Richie, who, quite frankly, could not generally organise himself out of a paper bag. The Thistles should have known better than to leave it all to Richie and trust him with the finer details, but hey, I was not officially in the band by then, so I did not get involved. The group had not played many gigs in the last few months, and the money was good, so what the hell. I was looking forward to singing on stage again.

Not exactly a stage, just a dusty pub corner by the loos. And no parking. It meant we had to traipse backwards and forwards in the cold and drizzle with our equipment. The New Tavern was not aptly named. Pretty run-down, sticky brown and orange carpet, hardly any lighting and thoroughly dreary. Chubby, rosy-cheeked Big Trev was pleasant enough, but my heart sank when I caught sight of the three old stooges sat in flat caps at the bar, slurping down pints of bitter, even bitterer scowls on their faces. Oh, and two rather smelly, great big dogs at their feet.

'Is that it?' I asked Ian quietly.

'It's early,' he answered, ever the optimist. One of the things I loved about him.

But it turned out that was very much it.

We set our equipment up, did a soundcheck, then a quick warm-up. Seven-thirty, the landlord was tapping his watch. He obviously expected a young, alternative, post-punk band to play to three old blokes and two dogs and seemed quite happy about it. Or did he think we were folk or country or something tamer? I looked at everyone's leather jackets, zips and tartan. No, we did not look at all folk or country. We just had to get on with it.

I went to speak with Trevor, just to be on the safe side.

'Anyone else coming along?'

'No, that's it.' He looked at me quizzically. 'You in the band, girl?'

He did not look too impressed. It was going to be one of those nights; I could feel it.

'Yes, I'm the lead singer, Delphy.'

He looked even less impressed.

'I thought you said you would fill this place?' asked Ben, ever tactful.

'Usually would on a Friday, but turns out there's a match on tonight, so I didn't bother putting any flyers out.'

Oh.

'You know we're a bit alternative?'

'You what?'

'A bit alternative.'

'I thought you said on the phone you were called The Thistles?' Big Trev looked puzzled.

The three stooges and their dogs were expressionless.

I looked over at Ben and Ian. It was going to be a long evening.

We decided to really go for it and gave it our all. Big, loud, punk numbers belted out, whilst three old guys in flat caps sat at the bar, downing their pints. It was as if they were totally oblivious to us. Landlord Big Trev looked on, his big, flabby arms resolutely folded. He listened to us without a hint of understanding or pleasure on his ruddy, chubby face. The dogs' ears twitched when we did the soundcheck, but that was about the only reaction we got from our tiny audience.

Once we had warmed up and livened up, I took the mic over to the old blokes and practically sang in their faces. Still no reaction. I even nicked one of their flat caps at one point and danced around with it on my head. Still, no reaction. It was certainly a tough audience. I wondered what we could have done to make those three listen up and get a bit involved.

Maybe a topless number? Perhaps I should have danced around with my knickers on my head? I wasn't willing to try and was not sure even that would grab their attention. It was Friday evening supping pints with mates at the local and that was the extent of it.

After what seemed like a lifetime, the gig was over. We bowed out to nil applause. I don't think they even realised we had stopped playing. Didn't get a free drink from any of them, the tight sods. We packed up and Trev paid us. Quite well actually, so some consolation.

As I walked away, one of the old blokes called me over.

'Not a bad voice for a bird. Keep practising, love,' he commented with a cheeky wink, as he handed me fifty pence.

'Blimey, I feel like we've just played a gig to a Hovis advert with all those flat caps,' remarked Ben, spot on as usual and laughing.

'Yeah, Richie, great gig. I think we'll probably leave the organising to someone else next time. Our street cred has bombed down to zero,' remarked an uncharacteristically negative Ian.

We all laughed about it in the van on the way home. Not sure to this day what the point of that gig was. I wondered whether the landlord was having a bit of a laugh and playing a joke on the old guys, putting on a band like ours during their quiet Friday night pint. Maybe he just wanted to get rid of them? Or he just loved our band? Or perhaps he was just getting down with the kids? I think maybe it was one of the first two reasons.

Anyway, we got paid, had a bit of a laugh and it went down in our band history as The Hovis Advert Gig.

Big Trev never called us again.

The crying bench

I saw some kids
At the park today
Smoking a bit of weed
Doing some drugs
Trying to ease the pain I guess
At the crying bench.

I sat there with you once
We talked about us as usual
Us and our crumbling relationship
I sat there more than once
All on my own
Crying, sobbing
Crying over you.

Wishing you were here
Wishing we could talk
Wishing you would call.
Not so different from those kids
Trying to anaesthetise the pain
Trying to fill the gap
Trying to ease the ache.

And when I have that pain
And when I feel that hole
When I feel I want to reach for you
I take a walk to the park
I look upon that bench
And I remember crying, crying
Crying for all we were not.

Ever since we got together you talked about taking me away for the weekend. How you would love to spend a whole night with me in a hotel, not just a few stolen hours in bed.

We could take our time over making love, curl up together afterwards, spend proper time together. Sleeping, dreaming, waking.

The weekend away never happened of course. Ben never seemed to be quite as free as when we first met. There was always some reason: too busy; can't spare the cash right now; not the right time; Jenny hates me being away from home; Jenny is unwell again; Jenny couldn't cope on her own. Jenny, Jenny, Jenny, sad, ill, little Jenny Wren with her feeble, yet controlling, claws in him.

We had also talked a lot about having a night out together, just like we used to, when we were young and carefree. A fun night out, with neither one of us having to go home early. We would stay over together, fall into bed at the end of the night out, have wild, drunken sex and wake up together the next day.

We were in a pub having a drink before you had to leave to go home. You had met suppliers not too far from Cowlington. You stayed later and told Jenny you had to take the suppliers out to dinner. You met me instead and we had a quick pub meal, a drink and a chat. The pub had a cool jukebox, full of our old favourites. The Clash, The Stranglers, The Cure, the Buzzcocks. We smiled at each other as we listened and started reminiscing about some of our previous nights out.

'Remember the kebab guy?'

'Dirty Joe?'

'And the moustache?'

'How could I forget?'

'We should have that night out we keep talking about,' I suggested hopefully.

'Yeah, we should. Hey, what about this place? I'd quite like to sit here getting quietly drunk, then take you back to a hotel and fuck your brains out.'

I laughed. Ben didn't often talk dirty or even flirty. I liked it when he showed that laddish quality he still had, despite being a grown-up, very serious businessman.

'Actually, there's a hotel just up the road from here. It's quite nice and not expensive. It's within walking distance. I stayed there once when I was on a teacher training conference.'

'Oh, really? Well, why don't we have our night out around here then? Let's sort out a date and we'll do it in the next month or so.'

To be perfectly honest, the pub was a bit of a dive, and I could think of better places to spend our big night out together. I couldn't help thinking that if anyone else had suggested The Frog and Bucket for a big date, I would have thought he was a bit of a cheapskate. I didn't expect champagne and caviar at all but, well, it's nice if a guy makes an effort and takes you somewhere special on a date once in a while.

Particularly if you had been seeing each other for as long as we had, it was serious and there were not that many "proper" dates. I didn't say anything, kept that to myself and nodded.

'Can I leave it to you to sort the hotel out then? You know how busy I always am.'

And you did it again. Just when I was feeling happy, snuggling up to you in a warm pub, listening to music, feeling like a proper couple, you did it again.

Maybe I'm an old-fashioned girl, but I really did not expect to book the hotel for a night of passion with my bloke. And I was busy too. Once, just once, particularly after all the let-downs I had put up with, all the absences, the detachment, as Ben buried his head further and more deeply into work, it would have been nice if he had simply said:

'Leave it with me, Delphy – let me know some dates and I'll book a restaurant and the hotel. My treat. I know I haven't been there for you these last few months. I want to do something special for you. Make up for your birthday.'

If only.

I said nothing because I did not want to spoil the evening. Nor did I want to appear demanding. And I did not want to upset Ben. I kept quiet again, but as I drove home, I was in tears once more. Crying because I was in love with a selfish man who just did not get it. Crying because I did not imagine that this was how it would be with him. Crying because I thought I deserved more.

The next day I walked over to my local park. I sat on the bench and my phone beeped.

"Sorry won't be able to message much today, too busy. Have a great day, message tonight Xx".

I switched off my phone and tucked it back in my bag.

Everything about my relationship with Ben was making me feel like a loser. I really couldn't be bothered to come up with dates for the hotel. I knew that if I did not mention it, he would probably forget about it anyway. If it did come up in conversation, I would say that no, I would not be booking any hotel for us.

Funnily enough, it never did. Because Ben was a dreamer and made flaky promises that were easily broken. If I wanted to stay with him, then I had to accept that.

Guardian angel

We had played a gig in the next town and were driving back in the van. It wasn't a bad night, quite a good turnout considering it was not on our home turf and on a Wednesday night. It was just after midnight. I was wishing I was tucked up in bed and kept thinking about the exam I had to sit the next morning. I was prepared but would have preferred an early night, instead of sitting in the van with a load of beery blokes.

'Oh God!'

'What now?' we said in unison, as we slowly ground to a halt in a thankfully convenient layby.

'We're a bit short on petrol.'

'How short?' I asked, panicking. I did not want to be stuck there all night with that lot.

'We've run out.'

There was a lot of effing and blinding and puffing and sighing. Then we tried to work out what to do. We had no idea where the next garage was. Or whether one would be open at that time of night. I kept quiet but silently fumed when I thought of the countless times I had asked whether we had a full tank when we were out of town or out late. I was usually told to stop fussing. Blokes!

'Well, we can't sit here all night – we'll bloody freeze to death.'

'We can all cuddle up to Delphy to keep warm.' That was Richie, flirtatious as ever.

'Piss off,' I retorted in my usual ladylike, charming way.

There was nothing for it. Two of us would have to walk it, try to find a garage and get some help. There was just a chance we would meet our Guardian Angel. Or there might be a working phone box somewhere and we could phone one of our older brothers to come and help. I was sure Neil would be thrilled about being woken up at stupid o'clock for his crazy rock chick little sister. Joking aside, I knew he would come and help me. He always did.

I really did not want to sit in the van and preferred to get moving, so I set off with Ian. We thought there was more chance of someone stopping if there was a girl present. I felt nervous and just hoped whoever stopped was decent and kind. I already knew that Ian was not exactly the kind of guy to have around when there was any trouble. A bit of a wimp really and not great with confrontation. Another minus point.

We were walking along with spare change for the phone and an empty petrol can. After ten or fifteen minutes, a car slowed down next to us. Hopefully our Guardian Angel.

''Ello, 'ello, me lovelies, what's cookin'?'

I recognised that van. And could almost smell the grease and dirt from the person in it. Dirty Joe. And I have to say that we were pretty pleased to see him and not some weirdo. Or, at least, he was our weirdo. The kind of weirdo we knew was OK.

Dirty Joe did not carry spare petrol. To be fair, we would have been very surprised if he had been quite that organised.

However, he did know of a "right good geezer" who knew of a guy who did. Or something like that. Driving along with Dirty Joe, and his stinky little dog, was not the most pleasant of experiences. He took us to a caravan park, hammered on the door of the "right good geezer", who jumped on his motorbike with our empty can. Not long later, he came zooming back with a full one.

He waived away our money, accepted half a packet of fags and a couple of cans from Dirty Joe, plus a leftover (most probably hairy) greasy, cold kebab. He went back quite happily into his scruffy caravan with a respectful salute.

We drove back with Joe singing along to his Abba tapes. His voice added nothing to the tracks and was painful to hear. Hilariously, when we finally got back to the others, we were greeted by them trying to get rid of a couple of tramps who had climbed into the van with them. They proved very difficult to evacuate. Ben and Richie were trying to pull them out of the van, shouting and looking quite desperate. Ian just stood there.

'Oi, guys, fancy a kebab?'

Dirty Joe lured the two old tramps with the promise of a couple of cold kebabs which they stuffed down, whilst we sorted out the petrol and all got back into the van. Joe even threw in a couple of cans of orangeade for the old guys. He was all heart. I just hoped neither of those two old boys swallowed anything nasty. You never knew with Joe.

'Knew those two old muckers when I was at school,' Joe told us. 'They had their own businesses at one point. Went under in tough times. Hard knocks can happen to any of us, I always say, so I'd never turn my nose up at anyone. Right, that's me, I'm off. Got a date,' he said with a wink and a wipe of his nose across his customary old, dirty jumper.

Joe never wore a coat, however freezing cold it was.

'A date? At this time? It's the early hours, Joe,' I remarked, thinking of how badly I was going to do in that exam in just a few hours.

'Little lady friend of mine. Likes a cuddle whatever time I finish work. Her husband works nights on Wednesdays,' he said with another cheeky wink.

'I thought you were married?' I said incredulously. That guy...

'Shall we say I'm a man of big appetites, little lady.' Joe winked at me again. Urgh. Just when I thought he was slightly bearable, Joe disgusted me all over again.

Dirty Joe. Unlikely Guardian Angel. Hugely unlikely Lothario, but he came to our rescue.

I managed four hours' sleep, and I didn't do too badly in the exam.

Christmas again

That night before Christmas
When we sat in the pub
Laughing and talking
I watched you in the hub.

I admired you shyly
You held my attention
I think at that moment
You captured my affection.

You always hid your feelings
Yet you prodded and pricked
Always winding me up
Yet my heart gave a kick.

And it's that time again
And I do have to ask
If you're still holding back
Will this now be our last?

We had a day out together in December. It would be our last for quite some weeks. Ben had not been able to take as much time off over the festive period as he normally would.

On top of that, he had decided to take Jenny away for a few days on Boxing Day. He had arranged for her mother to have Rachael, so it would be just the two of them.

I said nothing at the time, as I did not want to seem possessive or jealous, but I was a bit gobsmacked, to be honest. You never seemed to do anything like that together and had not for some years. I wondered whether you had started to feel guilty. I asked and you said no, you didn't. I did not ask you any details about the trip away, just asked when you would be back. But I felt gutted, on the outside, somehow slighted.

As Ben had decided to go away over the festive break, there would be even less opportunity for him to message or call during what would already be a difficult time. I still felt low about Jordan and the whole scenario at school, and I hated spending holidays without Ben. I tried to blank out that he would be with Jenny and Rachael, playing at happy families, whilst I tried to have a good time without him. I would have loved to have spent Christmas and New Year with him. The price that is paid. No one was ever going to sympathise with me, of course not.

The other woman, the evil temptress, the husband stealer. Why would he not take his wife away on a short break? It all seemed rather romantic, despite all he said. And I was sure that Jenny would read it like that. It felt like a smack in the face and yet another indication that Ben did not care for me as much as he used to.

He also told me that they had bought each other mountain bikes for Christmas. They had both decided that they should get off the sofa a bit more and start taking some exercise.

I envisaged them cycling along together, chatting, smiling, laughing. *How romantic*, I thought again, and quickly put on my smiley mask.

'Are you going to go biking together then, like a new hobby?' I asked, trying not to show how stupidly upset this made me feel.

He smiled a little uncertainly. I wondered if he knew how jealous and left out I felt. I hoped not.

'Sorry, is that not OK?'

'It's nothing to do with me really, is it? It's just that you and Jenny seem to be getting closer recently. You seem to be doing more things together now.'

Ben shrugged his shoulders and looked a little uncomfortable.

When we talked about our situation at the beginning of the relationship, I had secretly hoped that Ben would prefer my company and realise how much he had been missing out on a proper relationship. I thought he would want me more, not less. Was he tired of me already, or was the extra relationship too much trouble and effort? Had my complaints over the last few months about his casual neglect and off-hand attitude taken the shine off things for him? Was he bored of me now too, in the way he had grown fed up with Jenny?

He promised to try to call me over the Christmas break, so that it was *not so difficult for me*. Just difficult *for me* then? He said that I was to let him know if I was struggling. I wanted us to talk on the phone before he finished work for Christmas. He said he would make sure we did. We kissed and ended on a good note. As we were kissing in his car, Ben seemed a little sad and reflective.

'What's the matter, Ben?'

'I was just thinking, if you had gone out with me all those years ago instead of Ian, we wouldn't be snogging in a car park all these years later, that's all.'

'Maybe you should have asked me then, and not kept your feelings to yourself,' I replied instinctively, without meaning to sound unkind or bitter. He looked at me blankly and said nothing in reply.

We said our final goodbyes and I left for my train home. I walked up to the train station and sat on the five-fifteen feeling empty, sad and very alone. There would be very little contact with Ben over the most magical time of the year, and I was already feeling lost and forlorn.

I fixed my mask tightly in preparation for the coming weeks.

Dreaming

I had another dream last night. Two dreams. In the first, I was walking to my keep-fit class, and I kept dropping things everywhere. I picked them back up, tucked yet another object under my arm, but then dropped something else. At one point, I had a whole pile of clean ironing under one arm and kept losing pieces of my clothing as they slipped onto the floor. Bizarrely, the more items that fell away from me, the more I seemed to accumulate, until I did not even know what I had dropped.

Finally, as I walked over a small bridge, all my belongings, including the laundry, fell into a small, gently flowing stream. I stood there, on the bridge, looking hopelessly at all my stuff, all those parts of my life perhaps, just floating away from me. I ran from the bridge, ran into the stream and tried to retrieve I don't even know what. The objects seemed to disappear before my eyes. I looked around for some help, feeling quite distraught, but there was no one.

It felt as though I was losing everything I had ever possessed. I was also aware that I was late for my class, and this made me even more agitated. All my classmates were walking past me, not looking at me, nor recognising my distress. I felt bereft, alone, but also that I must somehow get to my class.

I walked into the building, without my bag or any of my kit, only to find that the class was now finished. My classmates had been going back to their homes. The first dream ended with me standing alone in the hall, wondering what to do next.

The second dream came a little later that same night. It was one of those recurrent dreams I occasionally had. They could be terrifying. During the dream, or nightmare really, I felt that someone or something was physically with me in my bed. It was almost like a dreadful visitation from another kind of being, not human, although it felt like a real person.

I was always sleeping alone when I had this dream. I could feel their touch, their presence, sometimes even see their face and into their eyes. It was petrifying – I could not open my eyes, move, scream, or shout. I could not physically push them away. I was in a state of semi-consciousness, half-asleep and could only lay there still, powerless, hoping and praying that, whatever was happening, it would soon pass.

On this occasion, I felt as if I was being held by someone big and strong, much larger than myself. The being was lying on the bed next to me and seemed very long – bony, thin feet reached beyond the end of my bed. I could see it was a man, a very tall, long man, naked apart from an undergarment covering his groin. He seemed attractive, with a well-toned physique. I thought he was quite beautiful in an ethereal, ghostly way.

I tried to see his face which was half-turned away from me, but I could not. He had golden hair, short and thick, sticking out aggressively at the front, and reminded me of one of my brother's Action Man dolls. A jutted jaw, very masculine, the golden hair was a stark contrast and a surprise.

Although I was curious to see his face, I was also very afraid. Something about his face was very dark. There was a blackness, a disconcerting aura of darkness around him. I was fearful that this was a demonic presence, an evil creature. I felt inquisitive, yet also terrified, to look him in his shrouded eyes.

He continued to lie next to me and hug me tightly, but it was not a comforting nor reassuring hug. It was a hard hold, possessive and controlling. There was nothing cuddly about it at all. I felt vulnerable, afraid. At last, and unusually in one of those dreams, I was able to speak.

I opened my mouth and asked of the long, blond man: *Who are you?*

He replied simply and immediately: *I am who you want me to be.*

I woke up with a jerk, sweating profusely. There was nobody there, of course. Those visitations, or whatever they were, did not hang around. They lived in the world of half-sleep and semi-consciousness. But I found they could bring messages. I lay there, feeling troubled, frightened and pondered the two dreams.

The first dream made me question whether the burden of my relationship with Ben was becoming too much for me. *It was about losses and gains*, I thought. I was beginning to lose bits of myself, gaining some small pleasures and happy moments, but they were taken away again very quickly.

The long absences built up and Ben would retreat and withdraw into whatever mood he was in. His moods changed rapidly, but he was often low, pensive, negative. I made some gains when we seemed close and connected but also accumulated a lot of pain, anguish and worry about Ben, his many problems, our future together and whether in fact we had one. It was stressful and unsatisfactory.

The long, blond man was telling me that physical and emotional connection was not always about love and care. It could be many other things: hard, aggressive, controlling. It could be about having power over another person, particularly if feelings are no longer equal, and one person had grown to love the other more. Or the other person just loved less.

More importantly, I felt, were those final spoken words. *I am who you want me to be.* Those words made me realise that, at least initially, we can fall in love with the image we have imprinted on another person. The mirror if you like. We love them because they remind us of ourselves or a particular time in our life. We make them into who we want them to be.

When I closed my eyes, I generally saw Ben as the younger version of himself, not the worn-down, faded version he had become. Ben showed me his best side when we first met up again because he thought he loved me, as he always did, and he wanted me to love him back.

When we were younger, I thought we knew each other very well, but we did not.

I saw Ben messing around, having a laugh, putting fake moustaches in kebabs, walking away angrily from yet another falling-out with Suzie. I always liked him and felt a bit sorry for him when he was upset. I felt flattered when he seemed to find me attractive, sought out my company and flirted with me.

But maybe, just maybe, I had not seen the other side of him. The side of him that was afraid of commitment, wanted to have his cake and eat it, as he so disarmingly told me himself one day. The side that was able to compartmentalise and push me aside to the substitute bench when it was convenient and easier for him. And when more was asked of Ben, and things started to become too serious, he grew scared and backed off. He became emotionally unattainable, unreachable, cold and distant.

The other side of you. And a side I did not think I liked.

Is love just an illusion really? Is it more about one's perception and maybe not about the object of our affection at all?

Was Ben just an illusion? An illusion based on memory, the past and who I would have liked him to be? My ideal, perfect match who had never quite figured in my life. Maybe there was a good reason for this? Perhaps my "perfect fit" was just a dream and could never be reality?

Was all that pain, all that wanting, longing and disappointment worth those few, random "lost in our own little bubble" days?

And what about Jenny and Rachael? Was any of this fair on them? However I had justified my relationship with Ben, deep down, I knew the answer to that one.

Cold

And it's starting to feel rather cold here
And I'm tired of not feeling warm
So I'm keeping my heart safe
Whilst it's only relatively torn.

And yes, I know that you're scared
And still so unsure of me
But I need to feel loved and secure
I just want you — can't you see?

And if you don't have the courage
And you can't be more sure
Then I'll have to turn away
Find someone who will love me more.

The run-up to Christmas was busy for us both. Ben messaged as usual. Boring, mundane texts telling me he had left for work and that he was busy, busy, busy. I kept waiting for him to suggest we talk, but nothing. It was now Thursday. The next day we would both finish at work for the holidays. If we did not talk then, Ben would run out of opportunities.

I hated asking you to call, particularly as I had already referred to it earlier in the week. However, I knew that if I did not mention it again, then there was a good chance that you would either forget or not be available. I felt uncomfortable asking you again and it hurt that you did not share my urge to speak. I yearned to hear your voice, wanted you to say that you loved me and would miss me.

"Yes, of course we should try to talk", Ben messaged back (only try to?). And he scheduled me in right at the end of his final working day. I knew he would be pressed for time or need to leave early to pick up Rachael or something. I knew it would be rushed, a hurried fit-in, a duty call. When we did talk, at least he was in a good mood for a change and not too stressed. He said he had some emails to send before he left the office.

That was Ben's cue to cut the call short, I thought. I was hoping for an indulgent, long romantic call, but I could tell he was in a hurry to get away. Get stuff done, beat the traffic. Always something to keep him from me, always something more important. Work, work, work, Jenny, Rachael, his own stress and then me. I tried so hard to be understanding and patient and accept the restrictions and limitations (so many!), but it was all wearing very thin. Last and least, whatever was left. That was my lot.

At the end of the call, I paused, waiting for him to say those three little words. The pause. Did he do this on purpose? I felt, once more, that as I put up with so much (and so little) and had to make so many compromises, Ben might have been more generous in his attentions. He told me he was not used to saying *I love you* so frequently. He said he did not feel it should be said too often over the phone or in text messages. It diluted the significance, he explained. And I should know he loved me, he insisted.

Really Ben? When I was getting so little from you, I should know that for sure, should I?

I told you I would miss you. It surprised me when you laughed and said you would not miss me always going on at you! That stung. I laughed it off but afterwards felt upset by your nonchalance. I found myself wondering whether we would make it past Christmas.

You had changed from last year when, despite everything, we had been romantic, close to one another and connected. I was in a fragile state, felt disconnected from you, uncared for and, most of all, did not feel loved or supported. I was starting to resent you.

Our relationship had changed for the worse and although I played my part in perhaps asking too much of you, you played your part in pulling back, taking my love and care without giving back. You drained me, at times, with your constant moaning and complaining about how hard your life was. However, when I turned to you for support, it was not returned.

Ben had drained the joy, fun and romance from us, but when I voiced my concerns, I was somehow made to feel that it was all my fault. He complained that I expressed my feelings too freely. He told me I was too open and needed to learn to keep my feelings to myself a bit more. Really? Did I need to change my personality to fit in with Ben's framework, his idea of how things should be? Did I need to become a diluted, less demanding version of myself for his ease?

Should I become a shadow, a wisp of who I truly was, would that suit him better? The ghost that his wife, little Jenny Wren, had become, perhaps? Was that what Ben wanted?

He's not worth it

The weeks
Turn into months
Turn into years

Nothing changes
They just seem longer.

The absences are gaping
The calls get shorter, sparser
A single line text message
Not worth the finger press.

The magic is slowly fading
As there's nothing more ordinary
Than waiting, waiting
For so very little.

That special something sacrificed
To its own fragile dreams
Flaky promises broken
Excuses are made

The tightening in the throat
Threatens to suffocate
As I begin to understand
What I always really knew.

One heart splintered
But not broken
Because it's all been heard before
And you really are not worth it.

You really are not worth it at all.

There's a defining moment in every relationship when you both know it is over.

It may take a long time coming, but it will come all the same. We had somehow survived Christmas; I'm not sure how. It took a huge amount of patience, self-control and discipline on my part. I expected very little, messaged sparingly. I kept Ben at an emotional distance. It did not feel natural for me, but I did it to preserve our relationship, for what it was worth.

It was a cold, but sunny, afternoon in February. We were sitting and talking in the park. We had made love that morning, then had a nice lunch. It felt like it used to between us before Ben started to become distracted, detached, self-protective. Whatever it was he became, anyway. He still loved me, he said, so it must have been something else, I guessed. Not me personally, nor his potentially dwindling feelings for me. I often thought that for someone so good at compartmentalising and "boxing" his feelings, Ben did not seem to cope with stress very well at all.

We were reminiscing about stuff that had happened during our earlier heyday years. We talked about a couple we knew when we were younger. Ben mentioned a party held by the guy, who was a bit of a nutter, when his parents were away. It was a few months after I had finished with Ian. Ian was away on a caravanning holiday in Dorset with his parents, so he wasn't around. Ben had gone to the party with other friends, didn't know many people there, just went along for something to do. He did not stay long.

'Yeah, it was really annoying. Couldn't get in the kitchen, the door was jammed shut or something. Some girl was being fucked by six blokes, one after the other. Bang, bang, bang... you could hear them fucking her against the kitchen door. We were all outside getting really annoyed – the beer was in the kitchen, and we couldn't get in there...'

I felt sick and a little shaky.

'Who was it... who was the girl... did you know who she was?' I asked.

'Never found out. Must have been someone from out of town... or maybe one of the girls from the squat. A couple of them were at the party. High as a kite. She must have loved it.'

'How do you know she loved it... or even wanted it, Ben?'

'What do you mean?'

'That girl. How do you know she wanted that and that she wasn't being taken advantage of when she was out of it and vulnerable? Raped even.'

Ben obviously hadn't thought of it like that. He looked at me blankly, as if he did not know what I was talking about.

'Why didn't you try to stop it?'

'What do you mean?'

'Why did you immediately think the girl was enjoying being systematically fucked by five blokes?'

'Six.'
'No, it was five.'
'How would you know?'
'Because it's not the sort of thing you would forget.'

Sad but no longer sorry

I'm sad but no longer sorry
That I had to let you go
Still a little raw, partly broken
It still hurts, just so you know.

I was living in the shadows
Coexisting in your dream
Living on hopes, disappointments
You were not who you seemed.

You kept me waiting in the wings
Wanting you to come to me
So many promises, so much absence
There's still a gap, but now I'm free.

And I've lost some of my sunshine
Some days I ache, and I feel sore
But I'm better off without you
You don't make me happy anymore.

At first you told me that you loved me
But soon you didn't seem to care
You made me feel a million dollars
Then left me drowning in despair.

Still a little sad, but no longer sorry
That I had to say goodbye to you
I'm no longer living in your shadow
Have my life back now we are through.

I had come home that weekend on a whim, having finished with Ian a few months earlier. It was hard to break it off. I had hated upsetting him. Hated that he wept in the car as we sat and I told him that I no longer had the same feelings for him anymore. I told him gently that I hoped we could remain good friends. We could still write to one another, hang out occasionally, go for a drink. I would love to sing in the band again from time to time if I was welcome. That never happened. Nobody, except Ben, seemed to want me around once I had split from Ian. Guys can be very tribal, I've found.

It surprised me that Ian and I could not be friends. I had always thought we would remain on amiable terms. We were such easy company for each other and had talked about so much together. But I also understood that I had hurt him, although I had tried hard to be kind.

He had waited for me whilst I was away at poly, but I grew away from him, became bored by him. I had fallen out of love with him, if I ever was in love with him – we were very young. Ian punished me by ignoring me or by getting at me whenever he could.

I decided to stay away from him, the band and his friends.

I had drunk too much that Saturday night. We were in a rowdy pub with a loud, unfamiliar crowd. Penny had gone home early, feeling a little worse for wear, and I got dragged along to a party. I did not really want to go and long regretted that I did. I was just out of a long, tired relationship, had too much alcohol, had smoked a little weed and all my defences were down.

We kind of gatecrashed the party. We were not even made welcome. I didn't recognise anyone I knew, just hung around on the outskirts, thinking I should attempt somehow to make my way home. Only problem was that when I tried to stand up my legs didn't seem to work. They felt heavy and lifeless. I giggled as I fell back into the sofa. The guy next to me had a neat brown beard. He looked at me and smiled in a relaxed way.

'Hey, take it easy, babes,' he mumbled, as he rolled another joint.

I could sort of remember making it to the toilet and then into the kitchen to get a drink of water, before I tried to ring for a taxi to take me home. I did not feel safe attempting to walk home alone and did not feel I could ask any of my new crowd to help. I wished that Ian, Ben, Richie or Penny was there with me. They would look after me.

I walked into the kitchen. There was a crowd of guys there. I didn't recognise any of them. I didn't feel I knew them. They looked older than me. They were all drinking from bottles of beer, and I noticed one of them snorting something. I tried to walk over to the sink and somehow stumbled.

One of them came to my aid and grabbed my arm. I smiled and tried to straighten myself, but he did not let go of me. He held my arm tightly and it hurt. I started to tell him to let go of me, but the next moment a large, heavy hand that smelt of fags, and vaguely of piss, was clasped over my mouth. The kitchen door was slammed shut. Someone tried to open the door, but they were pushed out and told to fuck off.

I must have blacked out because I had very little memory of what happened. I just always knew that there were five. I didn't know if they each took their turn; I just somehow always knew there were five in the kitchen, and they all seemed to be involved. Not one of the five tried to stop what happened.

I came to lying on the floor and crying, not sure of where I was, feeling dizzy and sick.

Some bloke was on top of me; my clothes had been undone, and my trousers and knickers were pulled down to my ankles. I could smell blood and could feel it trickling down my thighs. Suddenly, there was shouting, swearing, mayhem.

'Get the fuck off her! Get off her, you bastards! What the fuck are you doing!'

Someone threw a cloth, blanket or maybe a jacket of some sort over my pelvis and legs, placed an arm around me, asked if I was OK, placed me carefully in the corner. I was curled up, vulnerable and in pain, sobbing and confused. Not knowing what had happened exactly but knowing that it was very bad.

Two guys had sneaked into the party along the back alley, jumped the fence and walked in through the open back door, into the kitchen and stumbled upon a gang rape scene. Because it was rape and not a drunk, wild girl having a good time. There was a girl who had recently come out of a long, monogamous relationship. She was a bit lost and a bit upset, had too much to drink, a bit of weed and just wanted to find her way home and get some sleep.

She should not have drunk so much, but that can sometimes happen. She tried to scream and say no, but her mouth was clamped shut. She tried to hit out and stop them, but her arms were held down. Her legs were prised open. She was on her period, but that did not stop them.

They were drunk; they were hungry; and I was their prey. They behaved like animals. Worse than animals. Because animals look after their own. They were savages. I felt ill and needed help to get home to a safe place. But I was attacked, taken advantage of, badly used and violently abused.

The two guys who walked into the carnage were an old friend and an old foe. Keithie, for once not stoned, and Dillon. Yes, it was Dillon who covered me with his jacket and put me in the corner, whilst him and Keithie beat the living daylights out of four scumbags. The fifth had quickly escaped over the fence. For now.

Dillon dressed me; Keithie picked me up and carried me in his arms out through the back door. He kicked down the garden fence in fury, and they both took me round to my brother Neil's. My shocked and crying sister-in-law made me a hot, sugary tea and wanted to take me straight to the police station, but I could not face it. 'Please, please no,' I begged her. I didn't want anyone to know about this. I felt I had been drinking too much lately, put myself in a vulnerable position, had been stupid and paid a very hard price.

'No, no, this should not have happened; it's not your fault. They have to pay for this – they can't get away with it!' Sandy was horrified. She reminded me of Penny's sister at that moment. Protective, caring, furious and desperate for justice.

But I could not face the shame. I knew it would destroy Mum and Dad, who were so proud of me, so proud of our family. They would be devastated to learn about this. They would never get over the way their lovely, clever Delphy had been harmed. It would destroy them. I would become a victim in the community. I could never walk head held high again. I would not be able to sing on stage. I would always be the girl who had been absolutely wasted, off her head and raped by five men. They may have hurt and used me, made me feel dirty and tainted, but they were not going to destroy me.

Neil, Keithie and Dillon talked with each other. And then with Sandy. Dillon came over and reached out his arm towards me. I flinched. He understood and kept a respectful distance. He said he was so very sorry and would come by later the next day, just to make sure I was OK.

I did not think I would ever feel OK again at that moment.

'No need to get the police involved,' said Neil firmly. 'It's not what Delphy wants, and it's not how we deal with things around here. But mark my words, they will fucking pay for what they have done to our little sister. I guarantee the whole lot of them will be run out of town within months.'

Sandy ran me a warm bath, washed my hair and helped dry me with a soft towel. She phoned Mum to say I was staying with them overnight, as we had all had a bit of a night of it. *You can say that again*, I thought, as I overheard her speaking. She took one of her clean nighties from the drawer and popped me into their little spare bedroom to try to sleep.

She came back in a few minutes later with a jug of water and some painkillers.

'Take these,' she said. 'When the shock wears off, you will hurt – these will help you to sleep. You'll be alright, love, don't you worry. Neil is right – we will sort this.'

She leant over and kissed me goodnight and turned out the light. I'll never forget how kind and caring Sandy was to me that night. She just said and did all the right things. She listened carefully. She was pragmatic and did not judge.

That night was a dreadful night. It showed me how cruel, callous, selfish and violent human beings can be when someone is weakened and helpless. It also showed me the very best of human nature and how traumatic events can bring out the best in people. Neil and Sandra were amazing. And there was my old hero, Keithie, still looking out for me after all those years. And most surprising of all, my enemy Dillon had shown he wasn't really an arsehole after all. Dillon came up trumps. Double trumps.

The next morning, Sandy, ever practical, took me straight down the sexual health clinic for a thorough check-up and HIV testing. All clear, thank goodness, although it was highly stressful waiting for the HIV results. Thank God.

Sandy and I waited anxiously for my next period. It's unusual to fall pregnant when you're on a period, Sandra assured me. But you never quite knew. The thought of carrying the baby of one of those scumbags sickened me even more than contracting one of their horrible diseases. And then the thought of not knowing which one it was... I was never more grateful for the smear of blood on toilet paper a few weeks later. I thought of Penny coming out of the loos at the clinic a few years before. I told Sandy straightaway, and she shouted in delight.

'We'll do a pregnancy test anyway when you've finished bleeding, love,' she said. 'I've got one here for you. Just to be on the safe side. You've a bright future ahead of you. Don't want anything standing in your way.'

And the five? They paid a price for what they did. Keithie and Neil saw to that. Thankfully, I did not know them and never saw them again. The four who did not escape took a beating they did not forget that night. They soon gave the name of the fifth who thought he had got away. He sorely wished he had not opened the door to Keithie and Neil when they came knocking. All five were made to swear that they would never, ever come near me, look at me, or breathe a word of what happened to anyone. Keithie and Neil could look after themselves, and Keithie had some very tough friends who really did not give a shit, so the five knew what they were up against.

Dillon was also sworn to secrecy and told not to mention it to me ever again. He did not. We became friends for a while, but he moved abroad a year or so later. As far as I know he has not come back. We continued to exchange Christmas cards and the odd letter for a few years.

Keithie and Neil certainly took their very own form of rough justice very seriously. Neil found out all he could about the five, who they hung out with, which pubs they frequented, who they were knocking off, their families, what they did for a living. Neil knew everyone and was well liked and respected. Keithie knew the underground world and had time on his hands.

In a local community like Cowlington, word soon got around if there were undesirables in the area. Over time, the five found their work dwindled, as contracts were not renewed, quotes for work suddenly cancelled, redundancies issued. They were not welcomed in any of the local pubs or social clubs. Or they would walk in and see Neil, Keithie or some of his dodgy friends sitting there, staring menacingly. They would walk straight out again.

One by one, I was informed, they moved away to different towns where nobody knew of them, and they could start again. Hopefully, what they did would never again be repeated. I did hope so. My only regret about not going to the law was that they had formally got away with it and would maybe do it again. On the other hand, if they had been sent to prison, they would probably have been out in a few years anyway. Unfortunately, I have learnt that formal punishment in our society does not always fit with violent crimes against women.

No, we did it our way. And whether or not they really did learn their lesson, I will never know. But they did not get away with it, nor go unpunished. They were made to pay. Most importantly, I was able to walk tall in the knowledge that although I would always carry that trauma with me, it was private and contained, and I would not be discussed, pitied and treated like a victim by my community. I would not be defined by the pain, humiliation and torture of what happened to me on that one deeply regrettable, never-to-be forgotten night.

And then I learnt that you were outside that kitchen door. And all you were worried about was that you could not get any more beers. And you thought the girl on the other side of the door, whoever she was, was enjoying herself.

It did not even cross your mind that it could have been me. You did not know that I was there. But that shouldn't have mattered. It could have been Penny; it could have been your sister; it could have been Suzie. It could have been any woman who had drunk a bit too much, was in a vulnerable state and needed help. And you walked away.

Brand-new day

I don't want you
I want you to go
I'm shutting the door
Just so you know.

So sick of your voice
Always saying no
Sick of fitting in –
At your say so.

So tired of you
You're making me ill
If you can't finish this
Then yes, I will.

Chorus
Yes, it's all about you
Guess it always was
But it's not just you
So now I'm up and off!

You say this is love
I say no it's not
Time to dry my eyes
Wipe away the snot.

Take back your crumbs
Grab back my dreams
You're in my way –
It's a brand-new day!

I thought I would die
Now I feel more alive
You're out of my heart
It's a fresh new start.

Chorus
Yes, it's all about you
Guess it always was
But it's not just you
So please go, get lost!

Yes, do please go
You've had your fun
Time to get real
I'd rather be alone.

You're yesterday
Time to go away
Get out of my way
Must keep you at bay.

Go live your life well
Glad I'm out of this hell
It's a brand-new day
And it's beautiful!

Oh yes, it's beautiful

Yes, it's beautiful
I'm on my own and yes… (fade out)
Yes, it's a brand-new day!

The thing about being in a toxic relationship is that you don't always realise you are in a toxic relationship until you are out of it.

Sometimes, I think the worst man to be with is not the absolute bastard. He is easier to spot and, in some ways, easier to deal with. No, I think the worst person to love is the quiet and cold, hard and unfeeling one. The one who stops showing you he cares once he has captured your love. The one who changes once he has got you. Clams up, puts up his wall of defence, no longer shows his vulnerabilities and stops showing his emotions to you. He is scared and so concerned with self-protection that he is unable to love you fully. At least when you are dealing with a bastard, you usually know he's a bastard, and you sort of know where you stand. He doesn't pretend to be nice. He'll probably even tell you he's a bastard if you care to listen! He'll even be quite proud of it!

I don't think Ben is a bad man, but I do think he is a selfish man. I take my responsibility for having a relationship with a married man, but I do so wish he had just left me alone if he was going to back off so obviously once the excitement had worn off a little, and he realised he could not risk getting too involved. Just wish my heart had understood the message my instincts and my brain were telling me at the early stages of the relationship. But you can't help who you fall in love with. That kind of forbidden, passionate love can be very self-deceptive and may easily topple into obsession.

I walked away

Perhaps a little more fragile
But I could walk away
Through pain, through loss
Through blackness, through grey
I walked, just walked away

Finally, I woke up
Pushed away dark dreams
I walked into another day
I fixed a smile upon my face
And walked back to myself.

And I picked up the pieces once again, reinvented myself and got on with my life. I'd done it before and knew I would probably have to do it again. With hindsight, I didn't think the last couple of years were about Ben at all. Human beings are instinctively selfish, I'd learnt that much. Weirdly, I decided that relationships with other people were more about ourselves than the other person. I realised that they enabled us to grow and learn. They helped us to develop and transition to the next stage of our lives. The next era.

Relationships are about giving, taking, compromising, accepting. They help us to define boundaries, limitations, differences. How much are you willing to give of yourself? How much shit are you going to take from someone else? How much of yourself are you willing to give up? In Ben's case, not very much. In my case, I gave away far too much.

And yet, I survived. Broken, fragile and mourning little Jordan. Angry and railing against unfairness, injustice and the senseless events that take place at times. Often randomly, without reason and for no good effect. I still sometimes grieve for that dark, black night all those years ago and wonder why it happened to me. I ponder over what I did to deserve such treatment and how easily it could have been avoided. Wrong place, wrong time, bad mix of people, unfortunate circumstances. That's all I can come up with.

Meeting Ben again brought up a lot of stuff for me – trauma I thought I had buried and moved on from. But it turns out you can't ever fully forget your past because it informs your present and who you become. The past becomes a part of us, whether we like it or not. Imperfect, painful, uncomfortable as it is. It won't go away completely, despite any amount of therapy or tranquilising medications. I know – I tried. However unwelcome, the past will always come back to haunt us at some stage in life. It's always there in the shadows.

Those scumbags hurt me, of course they did. Married Guy hurt Penny.

But you hurt me too. You didn't hurt me physically; you weren't violent. You hurt me through sheer inattention and lack of affection. You came back into my life after many years and told me that you had always, always loved me. You seduced me with romance, dreams, flattery, with magical words. You made me feel so special, so significant, so deliriously happy.

And then you took it all away. Because when I loved you back, trusted you and gave you all my heart, you suddenly backed off and made me feel I was expecting too much. You took what you needed from me and then put up a hard, concrete wall. Because you knew you would never leave Jenny. And to be fair, you were honest about that right from the start. And I wanted you so much that I accepted the compromise and I never, ever asked that you did.

But I kind of naïvely thought that we would have our own kind of love. Our own relationship that did not need social construct or validation. It would be us, in our own little cloud of mutual love, support, friendship and tenderness. With Jenny and Rachael in the background, but not at the centre. Well, clouds burst.

And that kind of relationship, whether right or wrong, requires careful nurturing. Not just a few daily messages. It means making time, however *busy* we are. It means not putting up walls, defences and hostility when it's not convenient to have someone say they love you and hope to hear it back. It means not stonewalling when someone who loves you, and whom you profess to love, needs you a little more at times.

So yes, I feel let down and disappointed by you. I feel you did not turn out to be the man I thought you were and maybe, just maybe, you never were that man. You seem to have changed. You're harder, colder, embittered even. Your work, your family circumstances, your stale marriage that restricts, but does not excite or enliven – you have clipped your wings.

Where is the Ben who took to the stage, played to the crowd, held the room in the pub, was always there for his friends? I feel you have a certain amount of resilience. You go on; you protect yourself, don't let anyone in too much and so you don't get hurt. But you also won't grow; you won't develop; and in not allowing yourself to experience pain and sorrow, you will no longer experience joy. That is your destiny.

As for me, I got hurt; I broke – it took time, as it always does, to get over any loss or broken heart. But I got over terrible pain before, all those years ago, and I will get over it again. I have survived, yet my heart is still open. I'm not bitter; I'm not closed. Maybe more cautious about who I let in, but I will never, ever be defined and restricted by those who have let me down and hurt me. Because then they will have won.

I took a sabbatical after I ended the relationship with Ben. Working in special education is hard and being a teacher wears you down. I felt the loss of Jordan very keenly. It brought back memories of Keithie's death. I owed him a great debt, I always felt, and I tried to stay in contact, I really did. But he was a tricky character to pin down, and I wasn't comfortable in the criminal, druggy underworld he somehow found himself in.

I regretted I had not done more to stay in touch and maybe should have visited him in prison. I hated to think of him feeling unsupported and alone when he came out. But maybe he was beyond help and I would not have made any difference at all. Who knows? I certainly felt that Jordan had been let down. Keithie, Jordan – how many more of the different and difficult, the unloved and unwanted continued to languish in borstals, prisons, mental health institutions, care homes and homeless centres?

I felt totally depleted by the relationship with Ben. Worn down by the continual disappointment and let-downs. I needed to get away.

I had some savings, so I rented out my flat, gave up my job and went to Greece for the summer. I took three months out. Found a good deal in a cheap hotel where I washed up in the kitchen and waited tables every Friday to cover my rent.

I worked in a bar three nights a week at first and then managed to get a contract singing in a couple of clubs for extra pocket money. I didn't even dip into my savings in the end and still had an income from the rent from my flat in Cowlington. I was well-off and spent most days on the beach, swimming, sunbathing, reading. I enjoyed walking in the early morning when it was cooler and, later, sitting in shady cafés sipping coffee and local wines and eating delicious fresh fish and salads. I found a nice yoga class, did some drawing and painting, wrote songs and made new friends.

It was heavenly and just what I needed. It helped me to move on from Ben.

I did it. I got away from him. Finally.

Postscript: Ben

I loved Delphy; I really did. I always did love her and think I probably always will. I couldn't believe it when I bumped into her again like that. I always wondered where she was, what she was doing and what her life was like. She just seemed to disappear from my life. One minute she was always there; then she was gone. I searched for her but could never find her. Her parents moved away; no one seemed to know where she was anymore.

I would have loved to have spent the rest of my life with Delphy. She is so different from what I have. I love Jenny, but I am bored and tired of her. She is quiet; she is dependable; she supports me; she asks nothing from me. And I give her very little. I suppose I have just got used to it being like that.

In many ways, Delphy is my perfect woman. She is pretty, smart and funny. Kind of quirky and a bit eccentric, with the most fantastic legs and beautiful, longing eyes. You could lose yourself in those eyes. And I almost did.

I know I kept my distance. I know I stopped myself from getting one hundred per cent involved. I know it hurt her, and I know she felt I never did or said enough. But if I didn't keep control of my feelings, it would have been so easy for me to walk out on my family. Too easy to walk away into another life. And I could not do that to Jenny and Rachael.

I could not be that man, the one who walks away. Because I know what he looks like and I know what it feels like.

I'll never forget my mum's face when my dad walked out on us. He went out for a packet of cigarettes and never came back. Never even left a note. And took all the money we had.

Mum had a total breakdown, and I spent a bit of time in care. I was only five, and I never talk about it. I've never even told Delphy or Jenny. I sort of blanked it out. Mum recovered and got back on her feet again eventually, but it took a long time.

We never discussed those early dark times. It would have been too painful for Mum, so I never broached the subject of why my dad left us. She met my new dad a few years later and we moved to Cowlington. Everyone thought he was my real dad, and that's the way I preferred it. I still don't want to talk about what happened; it's too hard, and I don't want anyone's sympathy.

I love them both – I do. I look at Rachael's face when I tuck her in at night and I know I could never break her little heart. She's already had one dad walk out on her. It still gives me a little jolt and makes me smile when she calls me "Daddy"... I love it. I love being the one who can make her day just right, make her smile, make her laugh, make her happy, even when she is struggling to breathe. I hated seeing her in hospital on oxygen and I know stress makes her asthma worse. I could never hurt, upset her or feel I had contributed to her ill health in some way. I would rather sacrifice my own happiness than do that to her.

I love Jenny too. I wish she wasn't always depressed and ill, but she has also been let down badly in life and I won't add to that. I don't find her attractive anymore – why would I? She's let herself go, put on loads of weight, lost her sparkle, never wants to do anything or go anywhere. She looks and acts like an old woman, and she's only in her mid-forties. We have no friends, no social life together; everything seems to be an effort for her. She is not a happy woman. I have not made her happy, and I must take some responsibility for that.

But she has always supported me whilst I've built up the business and she never complains. Not like Delphy! Jenny keeps the house beautifully, does everything for me and looks after me. Bit like my mum really, I suppose. She's not interested in me physically either. Not got the energy, I suppose, or maybe she just realises I don't find her attractive anymore and has given up asking or suggesting.

We probably look a bit odd together, and I would much rather have Delphy on my arm. In some ways, I wish I could be more selfish and leave, but I know I am not that man. I could not let them both down like that and then look at myself in the mirror each day. I could not live with myself. And I think I would have ended up resenting and blaming Delphy. The guilt and shame would have tainted what we have, or did have – I feel sure of that.

The thing about Delphy is that she always wants *more*. She always did. She was always pushing and prodding, constantly trying to get more from me. She couldn't just accept that I love her but could not always see or speak to her. She wanted too much from me. But I also know that I was lacking.

I got scared when I realised how much she loved me and when I knew she would have been quite happy to spend the rest of our lives together. She was besotted with me, almost obsessed, I felt, at times. I know I drove her to that because I kept her short of attention and affection. I never gave her quite enough, but I did not do it on purpose; I really did not. I am not that type of man.

She even accused me of being a player once. Me?! She thinks I enjoyed playing games and that we were in a coercive relationship. The truth is, I was out of my depth. I loved and still do love Delphy. But I knew from the start that I could never be with her properly. I love Jenny, but I do not love her as much as a man should love his wife. Having them both seemed to be a way to patch up the missing pieces of my life.

I guess I didn't count on Delphy loving me quite so much. She overwhelmed me; she's such a life force. She's passionate, impulsive and full-on, all the things Jenny isn't. The sex was incredible, as I guessed it would be. I have torn myself apart regretting the past, wishing we had got together earlier, wishing I had never been at that party. I only wish I had been one of the heroes who had walked in on that dreadful scene and rescued her.

Delphy thinks I'm a coward, and she's probably right. I never even thought of it like that. Thought there was some sort of gang bang going on and some girl was having a great time. I was pissed, didn't really know how many people were in the kitchen, just heard a couple of vague rumours after the party. I didn't hang around for very long, decided it was not my sort of party and made a swift exit.

I can't bear to think that it was Delphy in the kitchen with those blokes that night. All those blokes, all over her, hurting her, making her cry. Doing what I would have loved to have done with her at that age, but not like that of course. I would never intentionally hurt Delphy. She has always meant the world to me.

But she makes you feel bad about yourself. Always picking holes – nothing I do or say is ever quite good enough. I know

I don't always get it right. The truth is, I'm paddling furiously beneath a calm surface. The business is in trouble and has been for quite some time; in fact, I may well lose it if I can't get more clients and buy a bit of time with the bank. I tried to tell Delphy this, but I don't think she understood, not really.

She thinks I am a work addict, and I probably am. It's a way of avoiding my life, trying to forget my stale, boring marriage, from which I have long departed in my head. We are companions; there is no passion, no attraction, no fun. Nothing like I had with Delphy, and I do miss that.

Delphy won't see or speak to me anymore. She's gone away again. Left her job, rented out her flat, gone off to Greece apparently. That's Delphy for you – when she's hurt, upset, had enough, she just clears out. I sometimes wish I had her free spirit, her bravery, her boldness.

And she's right about me in some ways. I'm timid. I'm all mouth and I lack her balls. She wouldn't have stood behind that door, wouldn't have cared how big, drunk or nasty the guys were on the other side. She would have summoned help, probably kicked the door down herself, and given those blokes what for.

Meeting Delphy again has made me think about who I am. I've always known my weaknesses but felt I was a good man. I felt I had integrity. I had forgotten about the party until I mentioned it that day. It never seemed a big thing at the time, just a girl who had a few drinks too many, having a good time at a party. I didn't hear her scream; it didn't sound violent, otherwise I'm sure I would have done something to intervene or help. I'm sure I would have. I had too much to drink and didn't think it was that kind of situation.

But ever since I related that story, it changed the way Delphy felt about me.

On top of everything else, it was the death knell for us. And I can't say I blame her for not wanting to have anything to do with me anymore.

If I had been in her position and found out that someone close to me had been on the other side of that door, what would I have thought? I didn't know who it was, but I thought the worst of her. I still can't believe it was Delphy in there, being treated so badly. It makes me shudder to even think of her being forced like that.

Because my Delphy, I will always think of her as *my* Delphy, is special, always has been. How dare anyone take from her like that; how dare they hurt her in that way? As Delphy said, how dare they do that to anyone? And it was just a few moments, but I stood outside whilst it was happening to her. Only a few moments, but I stood there and felt annoyed that I could not get another beer from the kitchen.

Not taking part, not listening, not jeering nor encouraging, but still I did nothing to stop it. I very wrongly assumed the girl, whoever she was, was having fun. I listened to other people, and colluded in a very bad misjudgement, whilst a young woman I worshipped was being violated and dreadfully abused.

In some ways, I think she was almost glad to find a solid reason to end it between us. She was becoming more and more frustrated by the lack of contact and the infrequency of our talks and meet-ups. I always thought of her as so strong and confident when we were younger. This new, more fragile Delphy took me by surprise.

She really lost it when that kid died. She said she thought I should have been there for her more. To be honest, I had so much on at work at that time, I did not have any more of me to give her. I felt so bad when she cried down the phone, telling me how much she missed me. But also irritated. I didn't expect nor want her to be like that. I have enough other people dependent on me. I always thought Delphy could look after herself.

I guess I thought that, for once, I could have it all. Delphy, my lovely Delphy, gave me the romance and fun I had missed out on for so long. And she wanted me too. It was unbelievable at first. But she's right – I didn't love her enough, and I didn't give her the care and attention she deserved.

The truth is I was terrified. Scared of losing myself. It was too easy to love Delphy. At one point in the early days, I could so easily have walked out that door. Then I would be just another man who walked out on his family when things got tough or were not enough. A selfish man who everyone would point the finger at, whisper about and never quite feel the same way about.

I would become my father.

If only Jenny would get tired of me or meet someone else. If only life could be that neat and tidy. But it rarely is. I'm ashamed to admit that when I first got together with Delphy, I found myself wishing that my wife would die. Yes, I wished that Jenny would die, so I could start again with a woman who seemed to be everything I had ever wanted. The sex, the laughs, the clever chat, that attractive energy Delphy always had. But thinking about Jenny dying just so I could have what I wanted… that was going into dark territory, and I pulled myself up straight. That's probably when I began to pull back on Delphy a little. I said I didn't, but she was right about that, as she is about a lot of things. I did retract a little, soon after she fully committed emotionally to me, and I am sorry for that.

If two people should have been together, it was me and Delphy. Unfortunately, I never had the guts to ask her after she finished with Ian. I wasted my time with demanding, soppy little Suzie instead. The timing was never quite right for us, and timing is everything in life.

And now I've lost her for good.

But I kept my family intact.

Postscript: heart

I have the heart
That takes what's wrong
And moulds and shapes it
To a song

It's hard to lose
What you have gained
And sometimes wisdom
Comes from pain

I ached so much
I thought I'd die
So raw, so cold
And asking why

I was bereft
Felt left behind
Thought you were good
So gentle, kind

But you're for you
And you're for yours
And still I loved
Despite your flaws

Forlorn, in tatters
Still, I survived
Like a phoenix
I rise, yes, I rise.

And still I sing.

Dear Ben

You won't get this letter because I'm afraid I can't have any more contact with you, but it's kind of therapeutic for me to write it all down, so here goes.

It's now eighteen months since I ended our relationship, moved on from your crumbs and being fitted in guiltily around work and your family. I went to Greece to think things through and to recover.

I took three months off and got away from you, us, my horrible, useless headteacher and all the sadness surrounding Jordan's death whose short, tragic little life seemed to symbolise the sheer pointlessness of life at times.

I bathed in the sea, drunk cocktails in the evening sunshine and met some great new friends. I even attended local language classes and learnt a little Greek. I really enjoyed them and learnt enough to order my meals and drinks and have a little chat in the local store. All good fun, and they helped me blend into the local community.

I have finally found Delphy again, or rather another new version of her. She seems to transform every decade, but maybe she is supposed to?

I even found myself a new man! He wasn't for keeps, but we had some lovely times together. And he most definitely was not married, so for a few very special weeks, he was all mine, and I did not have to share him. Not too good at sharing, as you know.

Anyway, I had my own life to get back to, a new me, and he also had his own life and a business to run in Crete. Alas, it was not to be forever, but I have a feeling that made it sweeter, as is sometimes the case. A lovely, uncomplicated holiday romance.

I managed to get another job in my old school – they were either desperate or no one else was daft enough to do the job! A lovely new head, thank goodness, more support in the classroom and a bit more money, so all good. I feel more appreciated, more respected and am better rewarded – it makes such a difference.

My flat was very well looked after whilst I was away; the tenants were exemplary – they even left me a thank-you card and a box of chocolates. They can come again if I ever take off for another sabbatical! I now have a new lodger in the spare room, Juliet, a young, newly qualified teacher and sometime babysitter.

Yes, a babysitter. A few weeks after coming back from Crete, I started to feel a little nauseous and realised I had missed my period. As I said, I did have a lovely time with Antonio!

I now have a beautiful little baby girl. I have named her Thea. It means Goddess – you can't get more iconic than that, can you?! She's gorgeous, but then I would say that, wouldn't I? She has her father's lovely dark olive skin and is extremely easy and good-natured. Also from him, I suspect! I am very lucky.

Antonio was, in fact, thrilled, offered to marry me straightaway, but of course I said no thank you! If it wasn't on the cards before, and it wasn't, I really did not think the arrival of Thea should have pushed us into a marriage neither of us particularly wanted or needed. Plus, I love

England, and Antonio loves Greece. I wasn't about to do another part-time, long-distance relationship. All that anxiety and separation distress!! No thank you.

Antonio is very supportive, however, and Thea will grow up knowing she has a loving father. He lives mainly in Greece, and we are not together anymore but very good friends. He does come over quite regularly, sends a generous monthly maintenance and keeps in touch with regular phone calls and letters. It's working out very well.

I work three days a week in school, job-sharing with Marion, my former TA, who upgraded her training and is now a qualified teacher. We work together very well, as we always did. Her kids are older and more independent, so I have cover if Thea is unwell or has any medical appointments. She is a reliable babysitter, if I need one, and Thea is adored by her children.

I now sing professionally two evenings a week, one evening in a large hotel, the other in a social club. Quite good money, and I love the variety of having different jobs. Thanks to Mum, who has been brilliant, Juliet, my lodger, and some very good friends, Thea and I manage very nicely.

So here I am, a mum. Not married, not in a romantic relationship but very happy regardless. Thea not only has a caring father, but she is also brought up and looked after by a whole network of kind, loving womenfolk. Not quite how I thought my life would be… I thought I would have met the man of my dreams by the time I was forty. Buy hey, it turns out he does not exist, or I haven't found him yet, at least. Maybe I don't need him?

I once thought you were the man of my dreams, Ben, but came to realise you were in a bit of a dream yourself. Ours was clearly not a relationship built on reality. It could *not possibly sustain the pressures of real life with all its complications, pressures, imperfections. You loved a certain side of me – the strong, exciting, slightly scatty and fun part. You weren't quite as keen on the hurt, needy and fragile Delphy. Remember her? She was the one who needed more love and support than you were able to give.*

Please don't worry too much or take it too hard, Ben. I also had an image of you from our younger days, based on nostalgia and romance. Unfortunately, once I came to know you again and properly, I found I did not like the other side of you and what you had become. I found you cold and hard, controlled and detached. This is the new you and is a side you have perhaps had to develop to survive your life.

It's not for me though. I need warmth, support and love. I will not apologise for that.

It turns out that there are lots of different kinds of love. My mother love for Thea pretty much blows my head away. I am fulfilled and content being a mother. I can give, give, give as much love as I wish to my little daughter, and I never need it back from her. She rewards me with a smile, a gurgle and burp! These small, impulsive and utterly genuine responses make my heart leap with joy.

Maybe I'll need more one day, but just now, just here and at this point in my life… this is enough.

It's a brand-new day – let's move on. I hope you are happy also and that Jenny and Rachael are well.

In the spirit of love and forgiveness,
Delphina xx
PS I attach a final song. It's called "Fragments" and it's for you.

Fragments

Life can be very hard
Leaves us aching, empty, sore
We've all had our hearts broken
Had our backs up to the wall.

I guess we're all a little fragmented
You don't get through life unscathed
It's part of being human
To have to learn to sit with pain.

But one day we need to stop crying
Though we ache and we're still raw
We sigh, sit up, dry our tears
A little unsteady, let down, unsure.

And we gather up those pieces
Stitch those fragments of our heart
Because we never lose our stories,
Woven into each new start.

We may even try to love again
It takes courage, but we do
Searching for that special someone
Who's patched up with fragments too.